The '45 Rising

My Story

The '45 Rising

The Diary of
Euphemia Grant, Scotland 1745-1746

By Frances Mary Hendry

SCHOLASTIC

While the events described and some of the characters in this book
may be based on actual historical events and real people, Euphemia Grant is
a fictional character, created by the author, and her diary is a work of fiction.

Scholastic Children's Books
Commonwealth House, 1–19 New Oxford Street,
London, WC1A 1NU, UK
A division of Scholastic Ltd
London ~ New York ~ Toronto ~ Sydney ~ Auckland
Mexico City ~ New Delhi ~ Hong Kong

Published in the UK by Scholastic Ltd, 2001

Text copyright © Frances Mary Henry, 2001

ISBN 0 439 99229 X

All rights reserved
Typeset by TW Typesetting, Midsomer Norton, Somerset
Printed by Mackays of Chatham, Chatham, Kent
Cover image: Portrait of a Lady, said to be Mrs Ann Bowney by Rev. James
Wills (fl.1740-77) Agnew & Sons, London, UK/Bridgeman Art Library.

2 4 6 8 10 9 7 5 3 1

The right of Frances Mary Hendry to be identified as the author
of this work has been asserted by her in accordance with the
Copyright, Designs and Patents Act, 1988.

Fourth Journal Book of Euphemia Grant, daughter of Duncan Grant, Merchant, of Crown House, on Castle Street, Inverness.

Tuesday, 3rd September, 1745
In the home of the Bailie Sir Andrew &
Lady Morag Lawcock, Edinbro.

As God sees me, I swear I shall never ever set foot on a ship again. Never.

I was so ill on the voyage, Captain Mathieson brought me to Aunt's house himself, & carried me up the stair. I near fainted in Aunt Morag's arms as she kissed me welcome, & puked on her skirt! Dr MacBeth, who lives above her, says it's not ship fever, just seasickness & bad ship's food. I must keep my bed for 3 days, & swallow disgusting potions.

Mother gave me this new journal book special for this visit, & I promised to write everything. What a way to begin! Shaming!

᠓᠌ᠣᠥ

Wednesday, 4th September

Uncle Andrew's a stout, square man, imposing in a crimson coat & brocade waistcoat. He seems gruff, but Aunt Morag reassured me: "It's no' you, lassie. Sir Andrew's one of the city's magistrates, out all hours with the other Bailies at Council meetings, for the town's in a panic about Prince Charles's landing, & all these daft Highlanders gathering to him! And when Andrew can't take his meals regular, his belly gripes him & we all suffer!"

Their eldest son, Andie, is in Frankfurt studying law, to join his father next year. Alan, 18, is tall, slender & elegant like Aunt, but dark not fair. He's serious & considerate, & sits to chat with me. He brought me a posy of sweet herbs – most welcome, Edinbro stinks! He's a corporal in the Train Bands – volunteer soldiers who drill & practise musket-shooting in the Castle yard every Saturday. For he's to be a soldier. Uncle Andrew planned to buy him a commission in the Black Watch last year, but Alan damaged his hip horse-racing. He still limps but he'll soon be fit to go.

The youngest son is George, 16, a sturdy brown lad, boisterous & noisy, but sullen – he's scarce given me more than 5 grunts. Alan commented, "Pay Geordie no heed. He dreams of soldiering, but Father means him for a minister."

I laughed – couldn't help it! – and said, "I never saw a lad less suited for the kirk!"

Alan sighed, & nodded. "We'd do better each in the other's place, but ye'll never change Father's mind once it's settled."

Poor Aunt had 5 other babies, but all died.

Alan asked if Mother had sent me here out of danger, with Prince Charles landing in the West to raise rebellion, & reclaim his father's crown from King George.

"No' exactly," I told him. "You know King George's army led by General Cope didn't dare face the Prince, but turned north towards Inverness? My friends & I were looking forward to meeting all his officers! But Mother declared, 'A lassie of 15 among an army? No, no! It's neither safe nor decent! You'll sail this day for Edinbro, to my sister Morag. You'll get some town polish & maybe she'll find you a good husband!' Parties, & the latest fashions, & no Mother? I didn't argue with her!"

"Aye, well, with the Prince & his Highlanders heading this way, Cousin," Alan remarked wryly, "you're like to find yourself among an army right here!"

Wonderful!

Thursday, 5th September

Alan brought me books from the Circulating Library, & an orange. Kind, as I'm no' fit to go out yet.

Aunt's delighted to dress me. "We'll have a fine time!" she said. "Your mother has sense, leaving it to me! Ye'll need 2 plain house gowns, & finery for the kirk & balls. Ye've £15? That'll make a good start."

"I'd thought it a fortune, madam. I'd get cloth for 3 gowns for £1 at home!"

Aunt Morag laughed. "Aye, things cost here! But bonny faces like yours need no costly stuffs nor fancy trimmings."

Gratifying.

She & her dressmaker, Mistress Nicol (she lives 4 floors above) got me up for a few minutes & laced me into new boned stays. I'll sleep in them, & the maid will tighten the laces daily. Aunt gave me apple-green broadcloth for my first gown. "A wee welcome gift, lassie!"

Very generous. But she's shrewd, she weighed the cloth before Mrs Nicol took it away to ensure she don't steal any.

Friday, 6th September

Up for 4 hours today. We're on the first floor of a tenement. The parlour bow-window juts out above the High Street & looks up right to the Castle & down left to a big arched gate in the city wall. The parlour has oak panelling, & yellow brocade bed-curtains round Aunt's bed in the corner, with fashionable swags on a pole above the window. Flowers are painted on the beams & floorboards of the rooms above. Aunt has a fine spinet with ivory keys, & plays well. I boasted of playing the guitar, knowing I'd left it at home. She's delighted, says she'll hire me one. Drat!

From the dining room at the rear of the house I can see over the lower houses & market gardens to the Nor' Loch, then over the hills to a distant silver gleam – the Firth of Forth. I sleep here, it has 2 beds that tilt up as seats during the day. Aunt has a rich Turkish carpet on the table, & Majolica china & 6 silver plates, & 4 Venetian glasses! The walls have new-fangled printed paper, bonny blue & white.

The lads all share a bed in Uncle Andrew's study. "When Andie's home it's like cats in a sack," Alan says. Uncle does most of his business in Paxton's Tavern – Alan says first & last items on any lawyer's account are tavern bills!

The kitchen's tiny & cramped with a wee grate for coal. Everyone burns coal here – it burns hotter than peat. By the door out on to the stair, there's closets for the close-stool & pantry & coal bunker. With shops so close, Aunt buys near everything as she needs it. She don't even make candles.

Nobody knows how old Mattie the maid is. She looks 100, & she's been with the family since before Uncle was born. She's tiny, just to my shoulder, & complains constantly, but works hard. She sleeps under the kitchen dresser. Other servants come in daily at 6. Joey Parrish (small, jovial, fat) is the cook.

Ben Minty lives on the sixth floor above – he's lazy but kindly, with a shocking scar on his neck that twists his head sideways. (As a bairn he was bitten by pigs in the street.)

Saturday, 7th September

My new gown's ready! Also 2 full starched petticoats. Gave my old gown to Mattie.

Went out with Alan to the "Promenade", when everybody walks out on the High Street to meet friends, noon till 2, while shopkeepers shut for dinner. The High Street runs down a ridge about 1 mile in all from the Castle to Holyrood Palace. Above us it's fine & wide & the Lawnmarket there is packed with stalls. But it's very narrow by our tenement, with the Luckenbooths (a row of shops) built right in the roadway opposite us. Narrow passages called wynds & closes, tunnel off thro' buildings on each side of the street.

Aunt's tenement has 11 floors, each with at least 1 family living there, from the caddies and chairmen packed in the lowest cellars to the students 3 or 4 to a room in the attics. A single stair runs from the yard right to the top of the building. Alan says some tenements have 14 floors! All the house fronts are painted brightly with signs to advertise businesses inside. Ours has a white pen for the writing teacher above us, a lawyer's wig for Uncle Andrew, a letter for the Post Office, a loaf & wine bottles & yellow cheeses for the 3 merchants, & white stays for Mrs Nicol.

The High Street's busier than Inverness, with shoppers, soldiers from the Castle, pedlars & workmen. Men trot about carrying shabby black leather sedan chairs. Everyone takes them, Alan says, to keep gowns & shoes clean. True, the whole town's filthy – pigs & dogs rootle in rubbish everywhere. Lasses milk cows into your own jug at your door, lads drive beasts & geese up the street to the butchers' yards in Fleshmarket Close. Caddies lounge at every corner, bundled in huge tattered plaids. They're all ages, from wiry white-haired ancients to gangling lads. They do or fetch anything you want, Alan says – they run with messages, carry goods on their backs, anything. Even fine ladies wrap up warm in silk-lined plaids – they're draped elegant over their heads. I'd expected cloaks & hats like London, but Aunt chuckled, "Edinbro's winds would freeze your earwax, lassie! Gentlemen here wear cocked hats, not bonnets, & the more important they are, the bigger their wigs!"

Astonishing pleasant to be treated as a lady by Alan's friends, not just "Duncan Grant's lassie". But soon I had to beg Alan to return, feeling shaky with these new stays, & the crowds, & the suffocating stink.

I was fine for Aunt's "4-hours" – a wee party from 4 till 8, where ladies & gentlemen drink tea, chat, nibble biscuits & play cards, regular every week. Aunt's are on Saturdays; other ladies have other days. These Lowlanders are so ignorant of Highlanders, & so terrified! I reassured them, "They come to the Warehouse in Inverness – that's a hall where our merchants have shelves to display their goods. The Highlanders are poor & proud but peaceable & most polite." They started to giggle at all my "p's", & that calmed them down. "What do they buy?" someone asked, & I said, "Only what they can't make. Tea & needles. Pepper & gunpowder." Those last words started them fluttering again, & Aunt Morag tutted at me for being a right gowk!

Sunday, 8th September

To morning service only, at St Giles Kirk. A vigorous sermon, 2 hours, about Gideon who was called to save the Israelites from the Midianites. It was really about King George's son, Prince William, Duke of Cumberland, saving us from Prince Charles & his invading Highlanders. But I heard whispers around us that Charles is like Gideon, saving his people from King George!

Uncle Andrew came home late from a Council meeting, gasping for ale. "The Pretender—"

"Who, sir?" I asked.

He huffed at being interrupted. "Prince Charles Stuart, Phemie, tho' he's no real prince. His grandfather, James VII, was driven out by Parliament 50 years back for being Catholic, for by law the King of Britain must be Protestant. James' son, Prince Charles's father, was never crowned. He's no' a king tho' he calls himself King James VIII, but he & his son pretend it's they should have the crown, no' King George II. Ye understand?" (I worked it out later, with Alan's help.) "The Pretender'll be here in a few days, with his Highlanders, & in the Council, the Provost is urging us to surrender! And most of the town's with the Provost on this. Some from fear of the Highland savages, & the rest are traitorous Papist Jacobites – even the Provost, aye, he is, I'll swear to it! Most of us Bailies don't want the Stuarts back, we're loyal to King George, but what can we do?"

I told Uncle Andrew about the whispers in kirk & he turned puce & snapped the stem of his pipe in anger! "Aye, that's the Jacks! The town's ripe to fall to the Pretender, tho' the Castle can hold out easy till Cumberland brings King George's army back from fighting the French in Flanders."

Alan hummed thoughtfully. "But Cumberland's still the far side of the Channel, Father."

Glowering, Uncle drained his tankard. "We sent warning south months back – but when did those prideful London blatherskites ever pay heed to a Scot?"

"Aye, well, sir, we must just pray General Cope's army reaches us before Prince Charles, to protect us." Aunt was worried. "Should we maybe go to your parents in Berwick for safety?"

"I think no', mistress. Ye're safer here than on the roads." Uncle grumphed. "Rebellion brings out all the rogues in Christendom! Thank the Lord Andie's well out of it!"

Will there be fighting? Here in Edinbro, even? Frightsome – but exciting!

Monday, 9th September

Shouting outside woke me. The Prince's army is near, & the bell-man was calling for volunteers to join the Train Bands to defend the city. Geordie, all sparkie, shouted, "I'm going!" Aunt protested, but his father gave permission. I wished I could join too. Alan praised my courage, but Geordie guffawed. Insulting!

Went out with Aunt Morag & inspected 11 merchants' stalls – such a choice of cloths! Feeling much better. Not before time.

Tuesday, 10th September

Chose light yellow printed chintz for a ball gown –
22 yards, for wide skirt & frills! And stuff for 3 other
gowns! And trimmings, & linen for underdresses, & a
fine silk-lined plaid. Near £12 in all! Fair takes your
mind off war!

Enjoyed 4-hours at Mrs Coslett's. Mr Coslett,
interested in Natural Science, showed us an experiment
in the parlour, to see how long a mouse can live when
the air's all pumped out from a big glass jar – horrid, but
fascinating! They have 3 daughters: Lizzie, Isa & Mary.
All lively & agreeable.

Wednesday, 11th September

We had a wee stramash on the stair last night. All
rubbish should be carried down to the gutter after
curfew at 10 o'clock, but most maids just open

windows or doors, shout "Gardy-loo!" as warning, & empty out bins & close-stool pots. "The Council pays men to clear it, but they don't strain theirselves," Alan says. True, you could scrape filth off the walls, never mind the ground, with a spade. And the stink! "Flowers of Edinbro", it's called.

Last night some College students from the attics above us were coming in late. They shouted the usual warning – "Hold yer hand!" – but Mattie paid no heed & drenched them! I learned several new curses. Is this what Mother meant by town manners?

Thursday, 12th September

A Jacobite mob rioted in the Lawnmarket early on, shouting, "Surrender! Open the gates! The True King home again!" & threw cobbles at windows. Ben was afraid to reach out to close our shutters, so I did & a stone hit the wood just as I latched it! Too quick for me to be scared. Uncle stormed, "The Provost'll no' take a firm hand with these Jacks, the swithering treacher!"

Later, Train Band Volunteers, mostly College students, paraded in the College yards. Our lads came home brandishing muskets from the Castle Armoury. Geordie pretended to stab us with his bayonet. I snapped, "You crimson rascal, put that by before I stick it where you'll no' see it in a month of Mondays!" He just guffawed. Alan's neat-handed with his musket, but Geordie's a menace.

Too dangerous to go out to Promenade, Aunt Morag says. Dangerous to stay in too, with Geordie & his bayonet!

Friends are invited for supper 2 or 3 times weekly. Tonight, 2 possible husbands for me came. Donald Rose, a promising young lawyer, & Sir William Needhold, a client of Uncle's who's incredible rich! Donald's cheery but spotty; Sir William's older & heavily handsome but sneering. Both very attentive.

Friday, 13th September

Letter from Father, with another £5 note! Uncle Andrew says that in uneasy times folk won't accept paper money, & bank officials are planning to move their gold into the Castle for safety, so he'll change the note into coin for me at once. General Cope is marching east from Inverness, seeking ships to sail back to Edinbro – going round the Jacobite army they say is near Perth now. Loyalist clans are forming Companies in Inverness to fight for King George against the Jacobite clans.

I'm going to an oyster bar tonight. Oyster-wives sell their catch in the streets, then hold parties in cellars to use up the rest before they go bad. Even lords & ladies go, to watch oyster-women dance in clogs, & join in. Sounds like fun.

6‍⁓‍9

Saturday, 14th September

Grand night! Clog-dancing's very energetic, noisy, & very bawdy! Geordie loved it, kicking & clattering like a madman. One man kissed me & Alan knocked him down for insulting me – I didn't think he had it in him! Their friends all piled into the fight. I & the other lasses screamed & laughed & cheered, till the oyster-wives slung buckets of salt water & shells over everybody! We crept in near dawn, dripping. Mattie, bless her, was waiting up to let us in quietly, & she'll dry & press our clothes. What a night! Nothing like it in Inverness – & no Mother to frown!

The Train Bands are ordered to march out to face Prince Charles tomorrow. Several lads slipped away, Geordie cursing them for cowards. Alan's solemn, determined to do his duty. Joey made macaroons for 4-hours, but Geordie ate them all because no one came, likely they're all too worried. My stomach's going like a butter churn.

Sunday, 15th September

Twice to kirk. Sermons on fighting for your faith & king. Inspiring.

Two Dragoon Regiments from the Castle rode out to face Prince Charles – very gallant, fine horses, bright uniforms & plumes. The crowd cheered, several wept & some (Jacobites) jeered!

Later

We watched from the parlour window as Alan & Geordie paraded in Lawnmarket with the Train Bands preparing to march after the Dragoons. It was thrilling, but Aunt Morag was distressed at losing her boys. Then someone on a grey horse shouted that Prince Charles has 15,000 Highlanders with him; that fair damped their spark! The Train Bands decided to wait, & join General Cope when he lands. All muskets were handed in to be returned to the Armoury – I'm relieved! Geordie's grumphy, but Alan's content. He'll do his duty, but he's not a born soldier – tho' I'm sure he's no coward.

Monday, 16th September

Uncle brought news: General Cope's army is landed at Dunbar, & marching towards us, about 20 miles east of Edinbro. Just then we heard shouting outside – crowds were running down thro' the closes. We ran to the back window & watched Dragoons on the far side of the Nor' Loch galloping off to join General Cope, not staying to face the Pretender! There's no one left to defend the town! Frightsome.

My ball gown's finished, very wide, dark green ribbon trimming skirt & sleeve flounces & lacing bodice. I look older – prettier. Dare I say a belle? Aunt Morag smiled, "Ye'll draw every eye in the hall!" Pleasurable, even amid this stir & danger.

Later

Bailies called to urgent meeting. Uncle says a letter is come from Prince Charles demanding the City Gates be opened to him. The Provost & 2 other Bailies are going out to negotiate with him.

We're dressed warm, all our money & jewels hidden about us, ready to hide in cellars or flee the town if the Highlanders get in. Aunt's grim, Alan bleak. Geordie's brandishing a carving knife & cleaver, regretting he's lost his musket. Poor old Mattie's trembling till she can scarce sit, let alone stand. I'm exalted with excitement, like Geordie. Wish my belly would stop whirling. Oh, my new gown that I'll maybe never wear! We'll get little sleep this night.

Tuesday, 17th September

Castle cannon firing 3 times woke us at dawn – the Highlanders are in the town! Mattie was in conniptions & screamed, "Oh, Lord save us, we'll all be murdered in our beds!" I said Highlandmen would never act so badly. I pray I'm right! Aunt gave her a sip of brandy to calm her & took a fair gulp herself. I wish I'd had some. I'm scared, but will never admit it, special not to Alan & Geordie.

Uncle, who went out for news, says Provost Stewart let them in! Some Highlanders rushed the City Gates as his coach returned from meeting with Prince Charles, & held them open for the Jacobites to march right in! Not a soul's hurt, thank the Lord.

Later

About 9 o'clock this morning, Aunt lay down on her bed, "Just for a wee nap." We heard shouting – "The Prince is coming!" Aunt was still snoring so Alan, Geordie & I slipped out to watch. They tried to forbid me, but I'd like to see the lad can tell me what I can or can't do! We borrowed the servants' plaids, not to be noticed, & joined the press of folk down the High Street towards old Holyrood Palace, where the Prince will stay.

Highlanders shoved a path thro' the crowd, just tramping along anyhow, all grinning & cheerful. Pipers followed them playing "The King shall enjoy his own again", & then came Prince Charles riding a white horse. He's incredible handsome – about 25, well-formed & fair-skinned. He wore a white wig, a tartan coat with gold braid & lace at the neck & cuffs, red velvet breeches, & a blue sash over his shoulder. Horsemen, mostly gentlemen in breeches not kilts, & some in cocked hats, carried his flag behind him. It was a red cross on white, with the motto "Tandem Triumphans" – Triumphant At Last.

The crowd were cheering, laughing, weeping & shouting, "Good luck to the Prince! God bless ye, sire!" We shouted too, so as not to stand out. But we were also carried away by emotion.

Then came more pipers & streams more Highlanders, some well equipped but many half-naked, like stunted starvelings. But even they were bristling with weapons – scabbardless swords, pistols & muskets, pitchforks, even cudgels. They had their women among them, gaping at the high houses as they swaggered along, leading ponies & donkeys piled with bundles – loot, most likely.

We returned home an hour after noon, sweaty & hungry, but Joey had gone out, so I cooked eggs. As we finished them, trumpets sounded in the High Street & woke Aunt Morag. Several gentlemen & 5 heralds in tabards embroidered in brilliant gold & red with the Scottish Royal Arms were at Mercat Cross not 50 paces off. When the crowd quietened, a herald proclaimed James VIII, Prince Charles' father, as rightful King of England, Scotland & Ireland. We could hear fine from the parlour window, as he read the Prince's declaration: he's come to claim his Father's Rights, not to oppress his people, & no one will be hurt

28

who don't fight him. The mob cheered, threw their bonnets high & fired a few muskets in excitement.

Geordie's scathing about Prince Charles: "Fine & fancy, all frills & lace, & did ye see the powder on his face? More like a lady than a man!" He minced about, waving his handkerchief, putting it to his nose to sniff the perfume – amazing comical! Alan was quiet, frowning. I fear he'd been impressed by the young Prince.

Aunt hasn't realized we were out, thank the Lord. Most exciting day of my life – so far!

Wednesday, 18th September

Loyalist redcoat soldiers hold the Castle for King George, but quietly, with no firing, tho' Jacobites guard the Castle gate to prevent any attack from within. Uncle's angrily triumphant: "I told ye the Provost's a Jacobite! He didn't have the Volunteers' muskets put back in the Castle Armoury, & the Jacks have seized them, now they've 5,000 good weapons to fight Cope!"

Yesterday a girl was hit in the head by a musket ball! Not a bad wound, & an accident, just those daft Highlanders firing off their muskets for fun. Many folk are leaving town – can't blame them. Joey hasn't come back.

Thursday, 19th September

I went out with Aunt & Alan – very nervous at first. Many shops are shuttered, but there is no trouble on the street. We met several of Prince Charles's officers, some Highland chiefs in plaids & feathered bonnets, all very gallant. They kissed my hand (first time ever!), gave me admiring glances & bowed with raised hats. But with Alan there as escort, there was no offensive familiarity. Aunt Morag perked up. "This may no' be as bad as we feared. They're gentlemen." She nudged Alan. "You'll need to polish up your manners, my lad!" He laughed. "I'll keep my tail up, never you fear!" I bought sheepskin slippers, & spun wool to knit myself red stockings – saucy!

Friday, 20th September

Prince Charles's army marched out this morn to meet General Cope. Uncle's pleased, "That's the end of the Papist dogs!" Alan said, "But what if they win, sir?" Uncle snorted in contempt. I'm sorry to see the Highlanders go – tho' I hope the Prince is beat, of course.

Sir William Needhold was at supper again, thick lips smirking, offering patronizing compliments – most irksome. Joey's disappeared, & he's not at his lodging – Mattie thinks he's joined the Jacobite army. So I'm cooking for now, with Aunt & Mattie. I enjoy it, with the fancy falderals here: oranges, cucumbers, potatoes, turkeys. But Edinbro prices!

Saturday, 21st September

During Aunt's 4-hours we heard hooves clattering on cobbles & I ran to the window. Four of our Loyalist Dragoons were galloping up High Street towards the Castle. A Highland officer shouted, "Halt & surrender!" They fired pistols at him, (one ball hit the wall right below me!) & rode on. He had to jump out of their way. Uncle said, "News of the battle!" & ran out. Returned dumbfounded. Prince Charles has beat General Cope near Prestonpans, in only 4 minutes' fighting! Alan shrugged wryly, "I did say the Prince might win." Uncle clouted his ear! The ladies went away all flustered.

No wonder Uncle's worried. Prince Charles is triumphant; what will he do now to those like Uncle who oppose him?

Sunday, 22nd September

Edinbro kirks are closed, the ministers won't pray for the Pretender. In one kirk, outside the town, the minister even prayed for his death, but Prince Charles just laughed & wouldn't let him be punished for it. Truly noble, Alan says, & even Uncle has to agree.

Wounded Jacobites are being brought in to the Royal Infirmary. Townsfolk are helping wounded Loyalists; the caddies have 3 hidden in the cellars below us, till they can smuggle them past the Jacobite guards into the Castle. Aunt sent Mattie down with money for them, & a bowl of stew. She forbade me to go – "No place for a lassie!" I slipped down anyway. I wish I hadn't, it was horrible. Stink & flies & bloody wounds! But they were so brave, not moaning in case they were found. They've terrible stories of the battle – Jacobites killing Loyalists as they tried to surrender, hacking them to pieces among the corn-stubble.

Many Loyalists are leaving Edinbro, including William Needhold. No loss.

Monday, 23rd September

The Caledonian Mercury says 500 of Cope's redcoats were killed at Prestonpans & 1,000 surrendered. It reports that the Jacobites crept up on the redcoats until "the closeness of our shot might set their whiskers on fire".

"Highlanders fire their pistols, drop them & charge, waving their broadswords & screaming like fiends – the devil himself wouldn't stand against them!" Alan commented. "Prince Charles sent surgeons for the wounded & stopped his men killing prisoners—"

"I'd hope so!" Aunt cried, but he shook his head.

"Some redcoats surrendered, but then started fighting again, treacherous villains!" Alan near knows the report by heart, he's read it that often. He says the Prince has offered amnesty to all Loyalist officers who swear not to fight him again, & welcomes soldiers who'll enlist with him. Many are accepting. Uncle & Geordie are raging, but Alan said, "How else can they eat? The Prince is generous."

"Easy for him!" Uncle roared. "He's getting trained

men, & who'll pay for them? Us! £15,000 he's demanding from Edinbro, & the same from Glasgow, & some from every town! An eighth of all our rents, too, and goods, clothes and shoes for his ragamuffins! He'll ruin us!"

Wednesday, 25th September

I picnicked with the Coslett lasses on the hillside above the Highlanders' camp, a popular pastime these days with ladies hoping to see the Bonny Prince! Everybody's wearing Jacobite cockades, white ribbon bows pinned on dresses & gentlemen's hats. "What fine skin!" Mary sighed when the Prince appeared; she was right irked when I hinted that it may be powder!

Isa interrupted, all excited, "Are ye going to the balls in Holyrood Palace, Phemie? Far better than the Assemblies!"

I mumped, "As a Bailie, Uncle Andrew's invited, but he'll not go. I'd like to meet a Prince, even a pretending Papist one!"

They giggled & Lizzie offered, "Ye might suggest that absence could bring Bailie Lawcock into disfavour?" It might work...

Thursday, 26th September

It did! Uncle still refuses, but Aunt announced, "For my husband's sake, I must attend!" Great self-sacrifice, she pretends, but really she's delighted. I'm to go with her! Tomorrow! Alan will escort us.

We spent this afternoon practising dancing, Aunt playing the spinet. Alan dances quite well, despite his limp.

Saturday, 28th September

I was too tired & busy to write yesterday.

The ball was marvellous! Aunt Morag was gorgeous in dark red satin & Alan looked older, distinguished in blue. What a crush! Fiddlers, pipers & harpists took turns, & there were wax candles by the dozen! Ladies put their fans in a cocked hat & gentlemen drew them out to pick their partners for the evening. I don't have a fan so I danced mostly with Alan. But twice I danced with Ensign Lachlan MacLean, a young giant, brimfull of vigour, glittering with a huge silver plaid brooch & buckles & weapons all over! He needed a shave & his hair trimmed, & I told him so. He laughed! I'll swear Alan was jealous!

Prince Charles danced 4 dances. He's very attractive, tall & graceful – & it *is* powder on his face! All the ladies were dreamy-eyed, & Alan's fair taken with him too.

Today the caddies chased a thief up the High Street in a hue & cry. He'll be hanged, tho' he's a Highlander, for the Prince is strict about looting, Ensign MacLean says. He came to 4-hours, fresh barbered. Aunt dislikes Jacobites & Papists, but likes bold young gallants, so she didn't know whether to frown or smile.

Sunday, 29th September

Kirks still closed. Uncle read Psalm 35, "Lord, fight against them that fight against me," & we all prayed most heartfelt.

Lachlan MacLean brought me a gift, a painted fan. He says Prince Charles is allowing provisions into the Castle. "Are you not besieging it, then, trying to starve the soldiers out?" I remarked, & he chuckled, "Months, that would take. Ladies can scarce be expected to be understanding warfare." Irksome – but he's hugely impressive, with flashing dark eyes & a lovely deep voice. I wish Alan was more like him in some ways. He told us that Royal Bank officers have brought the Prince the £15,000 he demanded from Glasgow, but because much of it is in notes they've promised to sneak gold out of the Castle, to pay in coin. Uncle's furious; after MacLean left, he snarled, "Helping that scoundrel to pay his army – it's flat treason! I'll stop that!" & wrote a letter to smuggle into the Castle with the food. Alan warned, "Sir, it's dangerous, what if the Highlanders find it?" But Uncle's determined.

Monday, 30th September

Highlanders searched the carts going to the Castle & found Uncle's letter in a butter-cask. At least he'd heeded Alan's warning & not signed it. Uncle's fuming about his bad luck, but I think they were told where to look. By Alan? I fear he's bewitched by Prince Charles. What will Uncle say? I pray I'm wrong; better keep quiet. Worrying.

Thursday, 3rd October

The Highlanders shot at carters taking in food to the Castle & the Castle cannon are firing now. Terrifying – I wish we could leave. Yesterday a cannonball hit our roof! The whole house rattled & the parlour window cracked. Mattie – & Ben! – screamed. Aunt just glared at the glass slowly tinkling to the floor & snapped, "Drattit!" I had to laugh – better than crying!

Saturday, 5th October

The cannons are stopped & builders are mending our roof. Highlanders & the Castle redcoats are exchanging musket shots up & down the Lawnmarket. A ball hit the doorpost right by Mattie – it could have killed her! Now we nip out thro' the yard to market – & to parties! Lachlan MacLean calls every 2 or 3 days – very attentive.

Wednesday, 9th October

A new proclamation was read out at the Cross: Prince Charles understands Scots anger at being ruled by England. He promises to repeal the Act of Union & make Scotland independent again. Alan's delighted but Uncle snarled: "Blethers! He wants to be King of Britain, no' just Scotland. And King George would never agree. Cumberland's bringing 8 battalions & 9 squadrons of cavalry from Flanders. He'll sort the Pretender!"

"More battles, sir?" I asked.

"Aye. A full civil war, like I feared. Thank the Lord Andie's away safe out of it all – I've written to him to stay clear & not worry his mother by returning." Uncle's gruff & peppery, but he does care for Aunt. He frowned. "Every damned rascal in the land is rampaging out, there's no' a traveller nor a beast safe!"

"The Prince has sent soldiers out after them!" Alan protested. "Anyway, they're thieving McGregors, no true Jacobites."

Uncle snorted, "Are you turning Jack, then?"

He meant it as a joke, but I fret over Alan's liking for Prince Charles.

All firing's stopped and Promenades have at last started again, now the High Street is clear. My hand was kissed 24 times today. Is Edinbro no' the place to be these days – if you're young & fair & well gowned?

Bank officials smuggled £3,000 in gold out of the Castle for the Prince. Uncle Andrew's raging!

Sunday, 20th October

Too busy to write these days, what with cooking, going to market & parties! Lachlan begged permission to call me Phemie; I said I'd allow the familiarity. I'm learning to use a fan effectively, & several Jacobite songs. Eleven Officers came to 4-hours yesterday! Alan's itching with jealousy – so funny to watch!

Party at Holyrood again tomorrow. Exciting, even amid all the anxiety.

Tuesday, 22nd October

Finest evening ever!

Alan shrugged when I said I'd put my fan in the hat, but he was peeved. I danced every dance! Introduced to more Jacobites than I can remember, including Cameron of Lochiel, the Prince's Governor of

Edinburgh. His fine reputation has led many to follow him in joining Prince Charles. The French Ambassador complimented me on my French! Three years' boredom at school, for 2 minutes chat – but worth it!

I was speaking with Lord George Murray (one of the Prince's officers) when Prince Charles himself entered, in a suit of tartan with a blue silk sash & jewelled medals. He walked round, paused to speak to a few here & there, & stopped by me! "Ah, bella!" he murmured.

"Mistress Euphemia Grant, Your Royal Highness," Lord George announced.

"Euphemia! A lovely name, for a bonny lassie! That is the Scotch word, yes?" the Prince said, a foreignness in his voice – oh, it just drew me!

"Aye, sir, I thank ye," I said, near too shy to speak – that's never happened to me before!

He smiled down at me and said, "Mistress Euphemia, pray honour me with your hand for this dance." Can scarce believe it, even now.

Just as well it was a slow Strathspey, I couldn't breathe well enough to dance a jig! Prince Charles is near 6 feet tall, dances most elegant, & his hands are incredible smooth. The candles were like a summer day, & the fiddlers' elbows going like grasshoppers, &

Alan & all my Edinbro friends watching me. Me, wee Phemie Grant, dancing with a Prince! He praised my dark Italian hair, & my bright eyes, & my fine complexion, & kissed my hand at the end. My heart was near choking me. Oh, it was wonderful!

Today I was very popular at the Promenade & 9 important folk called on Aunt so they could meet me & invite me to suppers & parties. Aunt's radiant with my triumph!

Wednesday, 23rd October

Alan's full of praise for Lord George Murray: "He's intelligent, forceful, efficient. If anyone can control the wild Highland chiefs & put the Prince on the throne, it's him!" He says Prince Charles pawned his own jewels in France to hire ships & soldiers for the invasion, but the ship carrying his men & guns was damaged by an English warship & had to turn back. "The Prince came on alone, with but 7 friends – was that no brave, eh?"

At the ball I overheard someone saying Murray's only joined the Prince to betray him."

Alan frowned. "Ach, Phemie, ye've misheard, misunderstood. Lord George joined His Highness's father King James in the attempted Rising in 1715, as a lad, & was exiled for it."

I nodded. "Aye & King George pardoned him on his oath never to fight against the government again. But now he's broke his word, to join the Prince. I'm no surprised they doubt him."

"Away, Cousin!" Alan protested. "The Prince has more sense than to believe that! Lord George is one of his chief officers." He grinned. "King George is bound to send an army to attack the Prince, so he's off soon, leading his army to the Border to fight there, but I think he's aiming farther south. English Jacobites have promised him thousands of soldiers when he crosses into England. France has sent men, cannons & gold & there's more to come. And the Highlanders swear fat Cumberland & his redcoats will never dare face them. In 6 weeks he & his father, King George, will be scurrying home!" He chuckled, but under it he's nervy.

I'm fair troubled myself, the way Alan's stirred by these Jacobites. Drat him, spoiling my pleasure with this worry over him!

Thursday, 24th October

Lachlan called again, vast & vibrant, & asked me to wed him. I near melted with exultation – & was desperate not to giggle, for Geordie was making faces behind him till Aunt glared him away. Tho' I like Lachlan greatly, I told him I've no plans to wed yet, & besides he's Jacobite & Catholic & I'm not. He started to argue – fair embarrassing! Uncle rescued me. "When these present troubles are safe past, sir, ye may approach her father to ask for her hand. Until then, be satisfied with her admitted liking."

Aunt's near dancing in delight for me, crowing, "Your first proposal already, lassie, after but a month!"

"Aye, but if Phemie was penniless he'd never have offered!" Uncle nipped.

True, I suppose, but still! He's well-born & a fine, gallant hunk! What a triumph! And more to come, Aunt says: "Your suitors will soon be queueing at the door!"

"Away, Aunt!" I said, tho' gratified. "I like Alan better than any of them." He blushed!

Saturday, 26th October

Alan was out all morn. He came in just before dinner & stood still & stiff before us all, in a blue coat with red cuffs, a red waistcoat, gold braid, & big horseman's boots.

"Sir – madam," he said, white & strained but determined. "I'm enlisted in His Royal Highness Prince Charles' Regiment of Life Guards."

Aunt screamed. Uncle cursed, seized his ebony cane & started to beat Alan, but Alan knocked it from his hand. They stood & stared, both appalled. Then, turning purple, Uncle bulled out & away down the stair, before he did murder.

Geordie helped his mother to sit & then stood facing Alan. "Ye'll follow that painted fancy-man? That Papist weasel? That—"

"Ye'll no' speak so of him!" Alan interrupted. "No' in front of me. He's our true Prince."

"True Prince?" Geordie snarled. "He's a fair-faced trickster, & you're a gowk. I always looked up to ye, Alan, but now…" He shook his head violently, spat on Alan's uniform & charged out after Uncle.

Aunt wrung her hands. "Why? Ye're going to your death! Ye know how your father feels – how we all feel. Ye'll break my heart, son. Why? Why?" Alan knelt beside her, stiff as if he was rusty, & took her hand. "I'm sorry, madam – Phemie – but I must. I just know he has the right & I must support him. I'm sorry." I held her while she wept.

I never said a word. I knew he was drawn to the Prince. I never dreamed of this. What can I do? Nothing.

I told Ben to hold the door, say there was no 4-hours this day.

Monday, 28th October

Miserable rows, tears & arguments – for we're all desperate to turn Alan back to sanity & safety. Aunt's like a ghost, Uncle raging, Geordie sullen. Alan's white, but absolutely determined to follow his princely hero, & his own romantic heart, no matter who he hurts. "He has the right to the throne," he says, as if that was a complete answer. Maybe it is, for him. He'll be killed, I know it. It will break my heart. I care for him – aye, I do. With all my heart. No' Lachlan, nor any of the others; it's Alan I love, with his shy smile, & his wee limp, & the way his long nose twitches when he smiles. Damn the gowk.

Tuesday, 29th October

Alan asked me to walk out with him this morning. He drew me over to Greyfriars' Kirkyard, where we sat on a gravestone to talk in peace.

"Just listen, I beg ye, Phemie. Don't say anything, no' for a minute." He was very solemn, pale, tired, but exalted. "I love ye, Phemie. Since the moment ye fell in our door, all white & ill." My heart near stopped & I was going to tell him I loved him too, but he set a finger on my lips. "But I must go with Prince Charles. I don't understand it myself, I just know this is what I must do. Like a command from the Lord."

He loves me, I thought & couldn't breathe.

"I'll no' ask ye to declare whether ye love me, no' so quick," he went on. "As long as you know how I feel. But may I write ye?"

I nodded, of course, forcing back tears, my throat too tight to speak.

"Let me buy ye a gift to remember me by?"

We chose a wee brooch with twin hearts like silver teardrops in a lovers' knot, & walked out thro' the Cowgait into the woods. All afternoon we just talked, or stayed silent. Or kissed. Sweet Alan.

I told him I loved him, too. Begged him to stay.

He said, "I've sworn loyalty to the Prince. Ye'd have me break my honour? Would ye wed a faithless man?"

Any day, if it would save his life; but I couldn't say so.

The brooch lies hidden in my box, in case Geordie jeers, or my friends. I don't want to tell anyone. Not yet. Sweet, sweet Alan.

Thursday, 31st October

I've had no time to write these days. We've been stitching like slaves – gloves, shirts & drawers & packing all into saddle-bags. Since Alan will go, we've equipped him as well as we can. Uncle bought him a good horse, Aunt a silver flask & cup, & I a new plaid, silk-lined like mine.

This afternoon I waved farewell to Alan, riding out among the Life Guards behind Prince Charles, very smart & determined. Lord preserve him!

I could scarce see for weeping so Geordie guided me home, arm round my shoulders, kinder than I've ever known him. He envies Alan and dreams of being a soldier too – but for the King, not against him.

Friday, 1st November

The last Highlanders marched out today, flags flying, pipes playing, better dressed & fed than when they arrived, & better trained & armed too. Many young ladies rode with them, wives mostly; I wish I could join them.

Uncle was grumbling at dinner: "What'll the Council say? Here's me a good loyal Bailie, & my son out for the Pretender!" I suggested, "Sir, in the last Rising in '15, when King James came over to raise rebellion as his son Prince Charles is doing now, many lairds sent one son to fight for James, & one for King George, while their father stayed at home to join the winner's side."

"Aye, so?" Uncle demanded.

I nodded to Geordie that it was time to speak up. He coughed nervously. "Sir, let me enlist in King George's army. Then the Council are more like to envy ye than condemn ye. I've no calling to the kirk, sir. It's always been my dream to be a soldier."

"Aye, sir," I backed him, "Ever since I came I've

seen he was unhappy, tho' he'd obey you dutifully."
Geordie flashed me a glance of gratitude. "But he'll
never make a good minister! And Alan's the same, only
in reverse! If – or rather when he recovers from this
daftness, he'd make a far better minister, or even a
physician, or a lawyer like yourself. I pray you, sir, let
them follow their natures!"

Aunt was distressed that Geordie would fight his
own brother, but we reassured her it's no' like they'd
ever meet. Uncle frowned; but at last he nodded &
grumphed, "Aye, well. Aye, well," & said no more.
Geordie's face is bright as sunrise.

Saturday, 2nd November

The Castle soldiers rampaged out after the Highlanders
had left – searching for arms, they claim, but really just
smashing & plundering. They've wrecked the Prince's
rooms in Holyrood, looted every known or suspected
Jacobite's house in town, cursed Cameron of Locheil's
wife & spat in her face. They even attacked the
Jacobites wounded in the Infirmary! Uncle refused to

go out; "Since the Council's dissolved, I've no authority, I'd be assaulted myself if I interfered."

I see why Mother wanted me away from soldiers.

Sunday, 3rd November

Kirks open at last! Our minister preached on rejoicing in freedom; suitable, now the Jacobites are gone. But I don't feel free to go out, because the redcoats behave far worse than the Highlanders.

Aunt declared, "I need a rest. We'll go to Berwick, visit Andrew's parents. Sir Andrew, ye'll find us a good ship." Geordie wanted to go & enlist right away, but Uncle declared, "Your grandfather was a major in the Glasgow Regiment, & may well gift ye his sword if ye go wi' your mother." That changed Geordie's mind. I said I never again wanted to sail anywhere; & that I'd stay & look after Uncle Andrew.

I'm writing to Alan every day. If I can't send the letters, he can read them all when he returns. Lord bring him safe home.

His brooch brings him close.

Friday, 8th November

Aunt & Geordie left early on the fifth. Busy as 6 beehives since then! I told Ben & Mattie, "We'll scour this whole house before her return!" They grumbled, "The mistress won't like it! Cleaning in November?" But I was brisk as Mother & told them, "I'll have none of your snash! If you're cold, work harder!" Promised them a shilling each which encouraged them vastly!

We swept the chimneys which were too twisty for a brush, so the sweep dropped a hen down the flues & it escaped in the parlour & scattered soot everywhere! We scrubbed the floors (all wood), whitewashed the walls, cleaned the paintwork, killed 1,000s of spiders! Uncle's keeping well clear.

William Needhold called, sniffed at my working clothes but pompously praised me as a good housewife. He sympathized with me for Alan's bad judgement in joining the Prince – which was more annoying than his disapproval – & explained he'd really wanted to stay & face the Prince, but he was needed at home in Roxboro. I told him I understood perfectly. Maybe he saw my raised eyebrows because he left in a huff. Cowardly big slobberchops!

Saturday, 9th November

What a morning! Mattie & I started the washing – tramping curtains, rugs & blankets in tubs in the yard with caddies & apprentices whistling at our bare legs, the cheeky rascals! Then a dozen redcoats marched in & demanded, "Where's Alan Lawcock, the damned traitor?" They thought me a maidservant with my skirts tucked up & old shawl. I didn't know what to do. I led them up to the house to show them Alan wasn't there, & Ben swore we were all loyal. But they saw the house was stripped & said Uncle had fled. They ransacked and half wrecked the house, knocked over Aunt's spinet & kicked in the lid, then beat Ben to make him admit Uncle was a Jacobite. Dr MacBeth came down at the noise & tried to stop them. They just jeered at the brave old soul, & he dottered off to the Castle to get help. They twisted our arms, slapped &

hustled us, kissed me & threatened worse. Oh, did I no' curse them?! I feared Mattie would let out who I was, & I'd be arrested as a Highlander, but she had more sense.

Suddenly Uncle Andrew charged up the stair waving his cane like Gabriel's fiery sword, & a redcoat Major behind him! Dr MacBeth found them talking in the High Street. Luckily the Major knew Uncle was a good Loyalist, so he came & called his men off, cursing far worse than me. Then marched them away, grinning.

Uncle was sore distressed. I sat him down & he told Mattie to bring out the Venetian glasses for Ben to pour us all brandy! At that, Mattie stopped whimpering & Ben chortled: "Those sodgers can come back any day!" We all laughed like jackasses from relief; then found they'd stolen all the bottles, the glasses & my purse! No wonder they grinned when they left.

"That gowk Alan!" Uncle grunted. "I knew he'd draw trouble on us!"

"Never fret, sir," I said, "We're no' sore hurt, just shaken." He gave the servants sixpence each & me £5 – more than I'd had! And Ben found a sherry cask the redcoats had missed, so we had wine after all, in pewter mugs.

I won't tell Alan about this, it'll worry him.

But who told the redcoats? Could it be William Needhold, in revenge? Surely not.

Sunday, 10th November

Day of rest, & sore needed. Mattie's shaking bad. Three redcoat officers held a dog-fight in the kirkyard after the service, in among the graves!

Thursday, 14th November

Loyalist cavalry & foot marched in, bright in red & blue uniforms. Crowds gathered to cheer, but fewer than greeted Prince Charles.

Sir William has called twice since the raid. I've no proof he betrayed Alan, but… Today we were refilling chaff mattresses which set him sneezing – so maybe he'll stay away!

Friday, 15th November

Letter from Alan! Post riders must still be travelling – astonishing. I'll copy it here in case I lose it – or wear it out with reading.

Near Carlisle, 10th November 1745

Dearest Phemie,
Forgive the scribble but I write on my saddle in some haste. I am well & in good spirits, as is the whole army. You see we have indeed crossed into England, under the Prince himself & Lord George Murray. Old Marshal Wade is leading 14,000 men from Newcastle to fight us; we are moving out momently to beat him before we face Cumberland and his regiments, who are coming north.

All the country folk cheer as we go by, but no sign of the thousands of English Jacobites who promised to join His Royal Highness at the Border. A sad disappointment. Prince Charles's courage & energy inspire us. He eats plain, rises before dawn &

marches alongside the men (keeping up excellent well even with the hardy Highlanders). He speaks & jests freely, the which does hearten us all. He is a true noble Prince, & worth all our love & pains.

Whatever comes, mind that I love you, Phemie, & ever will do.

Alan

14,000 men! When the Prince has but 5,000. And Cumberland has another army as well. Lord preserve Alan, amen.

Sunday, 17th November

The new redcoats seem more mannerly than the Castle garrison, tho' some officers think high of themselves, leer & hold our hands too long when they kiss them. Isa Coslett gave one the rough side of her tongue yesterday! But I can't be too sharp, not with my cousin in the Pretender's army. Very awkward. We've all sewn new cockades, black & gold or English red & gold – Loyalist colours, to replace Jacobite white.

Thursday, 21st November

Another letter from Alan!

Dearest Phemie,
Wade withdrew without battle, & we have taken
Carlisle! It was held by only 80 old invalid soldiers
& some local Militia, with 20 small, rusty guns.
Their only Intelligence Officers were 2 elderly
clergymen on the Cathedral tower with a spyglass!
I found a wee lass of 5 or 6 hidden under a bed. Her
mother thought Scots were savages & ate babies, &
I took great pains reassuring her. Lancashire is
promised to be full of Jacobites, & we have news of
many new men enlisting in Perth.

Unkindness grows between Lord George Murray
& the Irish Officers. They continual argue &
countermand his orders, the which drives him into a
frenzy nearly. Small wonder, when all goes wrong
& he's blamed for it! They whisper to the Prince
against him & I fear you were right, dear, clever
Phemie – the Prince does distrust him. It grew so

bad, Lord George resigned his Commission! But he is restored, for the Clan Chiefs will trust none but him, nor obey none other (& him scarcely!). His Highness is much offended & treats all the Highland Officers very stiff.

My nag went lame, & my servant found me a fine roan mare. He said he bought her for £2 but I think he lifted her from the stables of some Squire, as they call Lairds here. Dishonest, but necessary, I fear. I can't complain – he provides well for me: hot meals when I come off duty, & my gear kept in fair order.

I often think of you all. Mother's flannel undershirts are heartily welcome, England is as cold as Edinbro! I hold ye close in my heart, wherever I may go, as your plaid wraps me warm.

Your loving Alan

When I read parts of this letter to him, Uncle Andrew snorted, "I'm glad the gowk's well. But recruits at Perth? Aye, maybe, but the bigger towns are all declared for the King, & raising Loyalist regiments. Trouble between the Pretender & his officers, eh? Aye, well, I'm glad to hear it, but Lord preserve Alan." Amen.

Friday, 22nd November

A pair of redcoat officers called while I was preparing some broth. One dared to slip his arm round my waist, & kissed me! I chased the impudent rogues out with a mutton shank! Mattie emptied the close-stool out the parlour window as they left the close, but missed them – just as well, maybe.

Monday, 25th November

Aunt Morag & Geordie came home. I ran to welcome her; but she stalked round, stiff, unbending, peering at all the clean whitewash, shining wood, bright silver & cloth. Not a word. I was petrified. Ben & Mattie hid in the kitchen. "So," she hissed finally. "I keep a dirty house, do I, madam?"

I never thought of that. I tried to explain I was only trying to help, & repay her for the work & worry I've caused her. She sniffed, "I'm sure ye thought ye were doing right." Cutting, cold.

Good intentions are no excuse. I insulted her.

Thursday, 28th November

Aunt's rigidly polite these days. I burned the stew for supper; she ate in martyred silence. Uncle & Geordie stay out as much as they can; the Castle regiments aren't enlisting any new officers, they've no time to train them, but Geordie's determined to join & spends all his time there.

I wish I was home. I wish Alan was here.

Saturday, 30th November

Aunt was just beginning to relax; then Sir William & Dr MacBeth came to supper. Dr MacBeth enthused over how bright the house is, trying to help, but Aunt has turned all cold & hard again. William was eyeing me like he was a farmer in a cattle market, boasting of his wealth, land, houses, tenants. He's going to propose, I know he is! I couldn't live with that thick mouth, it'd be like kissing a carthorse. But he's arrogant & he'll take it badly when I refuse. Horrid evening. Men!

Wednesday, 4th December

Isa Coslett came in with Lieutenant Oliphant, (who's about 19 & an honest, courteous young man – for a change!) to invite me to supper in Lucky Andrews'

Coffee House. Isa whispered, "Mama always holds ye up to us as a model of industry & style – it's good to know you can get into trouble like us!" Aunt sniffed bitterly, but consented, tho' I must be home before curfew at 10.

Thursday, 5th December

Enjoyable evening. I was much admired, which cheered me immensely – & no William Needhold! There's a new political song from London:

God save great George our King.
Long live our noble King
God save the King.
Send him victorious,
Happy & glorious,
Long to reign over us,
God save the King.
God grant that Marshal Wade
May by Thy mighty aid
Victory bring.

May he sedition hush
And like a torrent rush
Rebellious Scots to crush.
God save the King.

Those who most cheered Prince Charles last month sang most hearty, to prove their present loyalty to King George. Just as I've changed my white cockade, I suppose.

I came home early, & Aunt nodded reluctant approval.

Sunday, 8th December

Sir William was ogling me at kirk, but I ignored him. The sermon was against vanity & fashionable dress in women. (A frivolous text, surely, during a war, but a change from vengeance & slaughter!) Going home, Aunt fumed: "Aye, men pay less heed to their gear – your uncle hasn't had a new coat in 6 months, he's more like a caddie than a well-respected lawyer – but that's no reason to scold at women!" Mattie scurried to make us tea, cackling. Aunt realized she'd been talking freely to me, couldn't in fairness go back into a huff & finally she laughed. We're comfortable again now – well, nearly. I must be careful not to set her off again.

Wednesday, 11th December

Geordie brings in news from the Castle. Prince Charles now faces 3 armies: Cumberland with 12,000 men, Wade's 14,000 near Newcastle, & more gathering to defend London. Lord preserve Alan, Amen.

William Needhold came to Promenade, but I was surrounded by redcoat officers. I told one I felt chilled, asked would he escort me home & left William scowling, black as thunder. Devil take him & his temper!

Saturday, 14th December

Letter from Alan!

30th November, Manchester

Dearest Phemie,
We walked into Manchester, crowds cheering us! But tho' Lancashire was said to be strong for King James, no more than 250 have enlisted, & some of them say they were out of work & would as soon have joined Cumberland! These are our first volunteers since we came to England, & some Highlanders are gone home. However, a letter is come from the Prince's brother Henry, that a French army will soon sail to invade England to help us. I tell ye no secrets, for the English must already know of it.

Lord George Murray has given up everything for the Prince, even his honour, & gets small thanks for it. He prevents O'Sullivan & the other Irish officers from bullying & robbing folk as they did in the French army. Also, they spur on the Prince to take any risk – they have nothing to lose, they can always return to France. But Lord George opposes them. He knows failure may see the Scots outlawed & exiled as he was. So they resent him, & turn His Highness against him.

Pray give my parents my love & respect. They may be easy about me – I have seen no fighting at all. I've never drawn sword nor pistol & my only wound is a scratched cheek from galloping thro' trees. (I must pay for my Army cocked hat & wig I lost there.)

By the time ye read this, we may well be in London! Dearest Phemie, if I beg ye, come visit London as my most honoured guest. Would ye consider it? Or even, dare I suggest it, as my wife? Our rapid success thus far in England makes me bold to hope for equal success elsewhere. My heart is ever with you, my fairest, dearest Phemie. I pray ye think on what I ask, & answer me kindly when we next meet.

Ever your most devoted & obedient Servant & Lover,

Alan

What shall I reply? My letters to him make a bundle as big as a Bible.

Later

Geordie charged down from the Castle with news. The Prince is retreating to Scotland! Uncle's delighted, but poor Alan! Is it good or bad news?

Wednesday, 18th December

Another letter from Alan, already! It came while I was out & Aunt opened it – irksome, but it's her right, since she's in charge of me. She was smiling. "I suspected ye were in love before he left, lass, when I saw the pains ye took with his gear. It's like him, to go at things backside foremost, courting ye just when he's off to the wars, & his father mad at him. No wonder ye kept it quiet. But ye must teach him to write proper love letters, no' army dispatches." I showed her my wee brooch; she has its match, the first gift ever Uncle gave her! "Aye, well," she smiled, "I suppose ye'll do for Alan, even tho' ye're feather-witted!" We kissed &

laughed together, for relief about Alan as much as anything. For he is coming home!

Manchester, 7th December

Dearest Phemie,
All our hopes are dashed to pieces. We reached Derby, only 140 miles from London, without any fighting. Some regiments of Loyalist Dragoons fled as we approached & left their dinner still hot on the table, for which we heartily drank their health! His Highness was joyful, planning his entry into London. However, we captured a Loyalist Intelligence Officer who said over 30,000 men surround us, against our less than 5,000.

The Scotch officers begged Lord George to tell the Prince we never expected to be his whole army. We marched into England only to assist His Highness, who guaranteed the English would rise for him, & the French would invade England & send us gold. But none of this has occurred, nor is likely to. The men are in rags & barefoot in the cold, & weeks unpaid. And if we did reach London, the mob there might well riot & destroy us. Our men need to plough their fields to feed their families next year

& some are slipping away to do so even now. All felt we must retreat.

His Highness shouted & swore at them, declared he'd rather be 20 feet underground than retreat, after getting so far & unopposed, & he believes many will yet join him. He raged special against Lord George that this was betrayal & treason, but the Chiefs were all determined to return to Scotland. The Irish officers were for advancing, & some few Scots also, but the Council decided after a full day of fierce argument that we must retreat.

His Highness says he will hold no more Councils, since he is accountable only to God & his father for his actions. He trusts none of us Scots now, Phemie.

I fear that our visit to London must be delayed. For the rest of my request, I hope to see ye soon, that ye may yourself tell me your wishes. Mine, ye must know. Only the loving thought of you keeps me from despair. That our great venture should founder, & so near its goal! I am that disheartened, my dearest Phemie, I can write no more.

Your Devoted Servant & Lover ever,
Alan

When Uncle Andrew came in, Aunt told him about me & Alan. I feared he'd want a titled wife for Alan, but he was agreeable: "All must wait on the future & your father's decision, lass, but as long as your dowry's sufficient – & I'm sure it will be, eh? Aye, aye. I've been thinking on what ye said, about Geordie & Alan. If Geordie's to be a soldier – & ye're right there, he's happier than he has been in months – then I can't in reason forbid Alan to study for a suitable profession once he gets this Jacobite foolishness out of his head. Ye've your head screwed on right, lassie. With his brain an' your good sense ye'll do well." Very gratifying – & not what Aunt said about me!

When he read Alan's letter, he looked pleased, but grave. "Aye, Alan's finding his Prince is no' the pure & noble leader he thought," he grunted. "Handsome an' glamorous, aye. But stubborn, no' determined, & little forethought nor good judgement. And he can exaggerate & straight lie like a horse-dealer. He'll no' trust the Scots, eh? But will they trust him? It's hard for Alan, poor laddie, to find his dream's but a bubble. At least he's on his way home."

Pray God Alan survives. His letters lie in my wee box, wrapped safe & tied with ribbon. If I lose this journal, I'll still have them. And my brooch.

Tuesday, 24th December

Uncle received a letter from a London friend. A French army is gathering in the Channel ports for an invasion, as Alan said. London's in a panic. King George has all his treasures packed ready to flee, there are riots & a run on the Bank of England, with everyone withdrawing their savings – the Bank heated the coins red-hot, it seems, to slow down the rush! If the Jacobites had gone on, could they have won? Uncle says, "Never, Parliament & the Protestant lords would have driven the Pretender out like his grandfather!" But I wonder.

The English officers sneer at us, as if we all supported the Prince. "All we can do is show them we're Loyalist," grumphed Uncle. "You're helping there, lassie!" True, I'm busy as 10 beehives, out to parties & suppers near every day. "God Save the King" is often called for – new verses appear daily. Latest one is –

George is magnanimous
Subjects unanimous
Peace to us bring;

75

His fame is glorious
Reign meritorious
Long to rule over us
God save the King.

Later

I left my letters from Alan out for 10 seconds, & Geordie burned them, damn the wretch! I cursed him, but he just glowered. I've copies in here, thank the Lord! But it's not the same. I didn't realize he still felt so bad.

Wednesday, 25th December

The Catholics & the English feast this day as Christmas. I was invited to 8 suppers & a ball in the Assembly Rooms! But Aunt wouldn't let me go to any, as it's really a heathen festival that was banned by our kirk 200 years ago, & she's strict. Geordie went anyway, I think. He was out for hours, returned flushed & tipsy, & went straight to his bed to hide from her!

We're steeping raisins in brandy for Hogmanay cakes & puddings. It seems odd to celebrate the New Year, when it's purely pagan, but the kirk chooses not to celebrate Christ's birth, because we don't know the true day of it. But hush! Aunt might stop Hogmanay parties as well!

Thursday, 26th December

Captain Mathieson brought in another letter from Father.

Phemie,
You have a good eye for fashionable fripperies &
knick-knacks, gloves, china tea-bowls & the like.
Procure them for me, for Captain Mathieson to
bring up on his next voyage. I enclose a note for £50.
Business is brisk, I am supply-master for the
army of Loyalist clansmen Lord Loudon is raising
here for the King. One Company is led by
Mackintosh of Moy, whose wife Lady Anne is
Jacobite; she is raising a battalion for Prince

Charles. She rides out with a blue bonnet like a soldier, & pistols at her saddlebow. The fools call her Colonel Anne. I fear half the town is Jacobite, among them many of your foolish friends.

Your mother has scalded her hand. Willie is well.

Your Obedient Servant, Duncan Grant

Typical Father. Business before all! But gratifying that he approves my taste & trusts me with such a huge sum, not to spend it on myself.

Other families have confused loyalties also, it seems.

Friday, 27th December

Geordie brings news as it comes to the Castle. Lord George, commanding Prince Charles's rearguard army, most skilfully beat off an attack by Cumberland's men – that will please Alan! The Highlanders crossed the Border back into Scotland on 21st, heading for Glasgow looting houses & stripping boots & shoes off every man they meet. In Dumfries they demanded £1,000 & shoes, & took the Provost & a Bailie as hostages for it all!

Uncle says the Castle Regiments should go and attack the Prince, but Geordie says they're waiting for Cumberland to bring up more men & take command.

Saturday, 28th December

The cook Joey Parrish is returned, much thinner. Very humble & no wonder – he'd run off to join the Jacobites, as Mattie thought. Uncle near kicked him back out, but Aunt said, "Better a gowk who's repented his mistakes than a greater gowk that thinks he'll never make none! And besides, we need him. We'll have half the town in on Hogmanay, & Phemie & I should look our best then if ever, & no' be sweating at the pots."

Joey has seen Alan often. He's in good health, it seems, and is well regarded.

I wanted to send my huge bundle of letters to Alan, now he's so near, but a kindly Post Office clerk warned me they're told to report letters to Jacobites. Lord preserve Alan. Amen.

Sunday, 29th December

We get fine, vigorous sermons these Sabbaths – I never realized so much of the Bible talks of slaughter & destruction!

Joey tells us the Prince is being as awkward as he possibly can on the way north. Lord George was ordered to abandon nothing, not even the cannonballs, which made an immense labour for his men. Tho' Lord George told him Carlisle Castle can't hold against Cumberland, Prince Charles insisted on leaving a garrison of soldiers there. He'd lie abed sulking till after 10 each morning to delay the army's start, & travelled in his carriage instead of marching. But crossing a river, Prince Charles stood 4 hours waist-deep in freezing water to help the men cross safely. "Aye," Uncle grunted, "he's brave an' hardy! If his head was as strong as his heart we'd fear him!" Glasgow refused his demands for gold & gear, & the Highlanders wanted to burn the town, but Cameron of Lochiel stopped them; the Bailies decreed that forever, whenever Lochiel enters Glasgow, the kirk bells will ring in gratitude.

Thursday, 2nd January, 1746

This has been the most miserable Hogmanay ever in my life.

30th Dec. Uncle was saying grace before dinner, when Alan arrived – thinner, in a brown wig & coat, not uniform. Such commotion & delight, Aunt weeping for joy! I could scarce breathe – nor he from the looks of him, nervous of the welcome he'd get. We dragged him in & only Geordie was stiff. Alan said he'd come by the mail coach without trouble. I set him in my place at table, & served him myself.

Uncle cried, "Aye, lad, it's grand to have ye home! And I'm heart glad to see ye in a plain coat!" Alan, supping broth as if it was the first he'd tasted in a month, smiled & nodded. "Mind," Uncle went on, "ye'll have to lie low for a while, until I can buy ye a pardon. But ye've seen the error of your ways —" Alan stopped eating & stared amazed. "Ye haven't? Ach, son, ye're never going back?"

"Aye, sir, of course! There's 5,000 men awaiting the Prince in Perth. Our army's in better shape than ever before. I came but to see you all. I'm no' so daft as wear my uniform here! But when I was but 30 mile away…" He looked at me. "I had to come."

I've never been so angry. Do I matter nothing to him? "You're going back?" I shouted at him. "I thought you were home for good with me – with us!" He shook his head. I slapped him, over & over, while he crouched away, covering his head with his arms, till Aunt caught my arms & held me. "You don't care how we worry for you. You're blind & cruel. I hate you, I never want to see you again! Wed you? I'd sooner wed William Needhold!" Shameful, but I couldn't help myself.

Geordie snarled, "Ye know what the Prince is. He's a trickster, a liar & he cares for naught save the crown. He'll sacrifice you an' all Scotland to gain it. But still ye'll follow him?" Alan was firm. "I must. I'd die for him." Geordie leaned forward, glaring rigid. "Aye, well, I'd die to stop him. I'm going to enlist for King George. Hell mend ye!"

"Geordie!" Aunt hit the table. "Ye'll no' kill your brother! Neither of ye will! Ye'll promise me, the both of ye, that even in the midst of a battle, if ye see your brother's face before ye, ye'll turn aside!" She reached down Uncle's big Bible from the dresser, & opened it where all his family names are written inside the cover as they're born & wed & die. "Swear it to me, here an' now, on the Holy Book, or I'll score out your name from it, & ye'll leave this house for ever!"

"Aye, I'll swear to that," Alan said readily. "I've no loathing for ye, Geordie, for I know that much that ye say about the Prince is true, & I know it hurts ye all, but – I can't leave him." He laid his hand on the Book. "I swear I'll no harm ye, Geordie, no by design, never."

Geordie jerked a bitter laugh. "Hah! That's right good of ye, Alan, for if I find you I'll put a bullet right thro' ye! Ye're a pure blind fool, & a traitor to your family that ye know ye'll hurt, & your country that ye'll rip apart, & your religion. I'm for the Castle the morn, to join any regiment that'll have me. If I can't get a commission, I'll enlist as a private soldier. And Hell mend you & your Papist Prince both!"

Alan was rigid with shock. He gaped at Geordie – we all did – & stammered, "But – but." Then his mouth firmed. "I'm sorry, Geordie. I didn't intend to hurt ye so bad."

I cried, "What about me? D'ye no' care how ye hurt me, then?" Uncle drew Alan off to the door, while I wailed in rage & despair against Geordie's chest. He held me gentle, trembling as much as me. They talked for a while in the hall, Alan & his parents, & then he left, his face thin & serious. Oh, my heart broke in me as the door closed.

That night, I couldn't sleep. I rose & burned my bundle of letters in the kitchen fire, every one. Mattie watched from below the dresser but never spoke a word.

All of us were very brisk & busy next day, cooking a grand supper, changing sheets, cleaning – not talking of Alan & trying to keep our minds off him. Uncle went out paying bills, collecting debts, to start the New Year fresh.

We had 10 in for supper. Last thing, Aunt raked out the fire & Mattie threw out ashes & every scrap of dirt, just as at home. We opened all doors & windows to let out the Old Year, let in the New. All candles were put out, except one; Geordie took it out on to the stair. As St Giles' bells rang midnight, we drank to health, wealth & happiness for all, & kissed.

Geordie knocked on the door & Uncle set it wide, saying, "Welcome the light of the New Year, & welcome him who brings it here!" Then Geordie came in, first-foot over the threshold, the tallest & darkest man there, for luck, bringing light to the house, & coal, brandy & shortcake, to ensure us warmth, drink &

food thro' the coming year. At home in Inverness the first-foot brings whisky, peat & salt.

Many friends called in, doing the rounds of first-footing, all very merry after mulled ale & wine at each house! Geordie went off with them. We had wine, music, dancing, 14 men kissed me under the mistletoe. I had a fine time! We got to bed near noon, then had more guests last night.

I'm invited to 5 parties this week. Why not?

I wish I'd remembered Alan's brooch when he was here, to throw it at him!

Friday, 3rd January

Geordie found an Ensign was leaving from Wolfe's Regiment at the Castle, & persuaded Major Wolfe to let him buy the man's place. It seems it don't matter how foolish or incompetent you are – if you're rich enough you can buy each rank from Ensign to Colonel & sell the rank you're leaving to help pay for your next step up. If Geordie ever reaches Colonel, he'll have paid £2,000! Plus his uniforms, horses, & mess bills that his pay will scarce cover. Soldiers depend on loot, he says, to make a living. But it's fighting he wants, no' plunder.

An officer came round saying more regiments are arriving. We'll have to put up 2 officers & 10 private soldiers. Mattie's in conniptions, Aunt's peeved & I'm worried – soldiers living in the house? The redcoat officers at the Promenade are bad enough.

Uncle looked very grim, went out & bought me a wee pistol – "Just in case, lassie!" But could I get it out & cock it, before an attacker noticed? Besides, anyone found with firearms is shot as a Jacobite traitor. I hid it in my box – now I'm more nervous than before!

Sunday, 5th January

This morning's sermon was about Moses commanding the Israelites to kill all male enemies, even children, & all married women. I'm fair sickened with the kirk urging us on to blood and war, as if there wasn't enough of it.

Tuesday, 7th January

General Hawley arrived in Edinbro with 10 battalions of redcoats & more cavalry. He's a small man, about 70, brave but harsh they say – & sneering at us as he rode by.

Two officers are sleeping in the dining room, & the men in the kitchen. I've moved to the parlour bed with Aunt & Uncle Andrew. Mattie's on a rug beside us, so she's safe enough – just cursing the extra work! Lizzie Coslett came in, raging. It seems their soldiers knocked out a pipe on a rug, started a fire, & pished on it to put it out, laughing themselves silly. Dirty swine.

The redcoats are jubilant – Carlisle Castle has surrendered to Cumberland. Prince Charles is moving north to Stirling. Alan will be with him – good riddance!

A letter came from Alan. I burned it, unopened, & had a fine time at the Assembly last night. I danced every dance! They asked me to sing. I refused of course – a private party is one thing, but not in public. Aunt hinted I shouldn't go out to parties so often. I said, "Madam, if I was betrothed, of course I'd no' dream of it!" She's wretched. Damn Alan!

Saturday, 11th January

Someone has told our officers Alan has joined the Jacobites. I suspect William Needhold again because I'm avoiding him. Curse him! I've no proof, & Alan's actions are well known among our friends, but... These redcoats despise the Scots, just like Hawley does. Now they're worse than ever. They complained we had no wine & when I said their men stole it, they laughed. I offered them buttermilk to annoy them & it did. Satisfying! One tried to kiss me so I slapped his face & told him he should be ashamed of himself – not the action of a gentleman. They laughed, saluted me, & may behave better in future. (Not hard.) I may need that pistol yet!

Even the ordinary soldiers roar orders at us as if this was an inn. They spit everywhere, leave boot marks & burns from pipes all over the table. One fool tried to heat wine on the fire in a pewter mug, & melted it. We've bought in wooden plates & leather tankards for them to use instead.

Geordie's new uniform has arrived – red coat with

black cuffs & white braiding, yellow waistcoat & breeches. Very smart, much admired by the ladies at 4-hours. But he admires Hawley: "He's a tartar, he loves floggings & executions, he's put up 2 gallows already. They call him Hangman Hawley!" Ugh!

Monday, 13th January

We went to cheer Geordie's regiment marching out to drive Prince Charles away from Stirling. Aunt was very down. Then, when we came in, we found our redcoats bundling all the silver & plates in the curtains & the feather quilts! Mattie was near unconscious – they'd hit her when she faced up to them, brave old soul! Aunt protested, "We're loyal subjects of King George!" They jeered, "Scotchies is traitors! The sooner we wipe out your whole cursed tribe of turncoat savages the safer us decent people will be!" We couldn't stop them carrying it all away. Decent people? Damned rogues!

Aunt's fuming with rage & frustration. At least we're still alive. Even Mattie was alright once we gave her a drink of ale. Then she produced the silver teaspoons from breast of her gown, with such triumph! We had to laugh. But we're all shaken & upset. We're robbed, tho' we're Loyalists – what will happen to Jacobite families? Uncle's furious & disgusted: "Complain? Ach, who'd listen?"

The house feels empty now, but safer.

Wednesday, 15th January

Mattie never wakened this morning. She died quiet in her sleep, curled in her wee bed under the dresser. Too many shocks. Poor old wife.

Aunt comforted me as I wept, "She had a long life & died peaceful among her own folk. What more can a body want? Don't mourn her too sore, lassie, she'd never want ye sad, but remember her." I shall do.

☙

Saturday, 18th January

We all attended Mattie's funeral service & Uncle himself went to the graveside to honour her — she'd been in the family since before he was born. He bought her a good grave, with only 3 others in it. Lord have mercy on her faithful, cantankerous old soul.

More regiments arrived at the castle, & artillery. The house shook from the cannons rattling up the cobbled street — deafening!

Sunday, 19th January

After kirk, there were whispers of a battle yesterday at Falkirk in terrible storm & darkness. Two of Hawley's cavalry regiments broke & ran from a Highland charge. They rode right over the Glasgow Regiment behind them & killed several men. Many of

Hawley's men fled – Wolfe's Regiment among them, we hear – but others stood fast or even advanced. Aunt's been praying all day, & I too – only for Geordie, of course.

Monday, 20th January

At Promenade, William Needhold sneered that very few redcoats were killed because they ran away too fast. Some even commandeered a ship in Bo'ness to escape! (He'd have stood firm, of course, if he'd been there!) Uncle said if there's no news of his son by the morn he'll go himself to Hawley's camp.

But later, Lieutenant Oliphant was riding up to the Castle, his arm in a sling. I called to him from the parlour window & he said Geordie's unhurt. Myself & Aunt were near weeping with relief. I don't care what happens to Alan. No I don't!

We've a new maid – Nellie, Ben's niece. She's about 10 & a sparkie wee lass, but ignorant about working in a genteel house. She'll learn.

Thursday, 23rd January

Letter from Geordie. Atrocious writing, & spelling,
I'll correct it as I copy it.

Falkirk, 20th Jan

Dear Father,
I'm well, tho' my red coat has shrunk
uncomfortable tight with the storm and rain, and
my shirt is dyed bright pink! The Dragoons on our
left broke and fled, & the right of the army stood
firm against the Highlanders' charge. But where we
were was all confusion & since our cartridges were
soaked so that we couldn't fire our muskets, we had
to run too or be flanked.

(Flanked means attacked from the side, Uncle
explained. Very dangerous. But maybe Geordie's just
putting the best face on it!)

General Hawley swears he'll hang 60 men for cowardice & desertion.

Next night I joined a dozen local men for a venture. We crept west to a tower where Loyalist officers had been imprisoned since the fight at Prestonpans. At dawn we knocked on the door & the doorkeeper opened to us, easy as that. Should have seen his face when he saw our uniforms! We rescued 31 officers & locked the gaolers in their place. We scurried back to camp, dodging Jacks, & were welcomed like heroes, tho' it was a mere lark, but Major Wolfe says it has lifted all our spirits after the shambles of the battle.

Regards to Phemie, & all my friends.

Your loving son, George

Uncle's delighted that Geordie has distinguished himself already, but grumbled, "Who else would be daft enough for such a caper?"

Saturday, 25th January

William Needhold, at supper, declared most condescending that his father will allow him to marry me! But William's like an ill-trained dog, he might well bite, so I was most polite & said he'd have to ask my father, much as I said to Lachlan – only 2 months ago. (It seems like years!) William smiled patronizingly, said he was glad I'm modest & shy, as in the good old days. Gowk!

Lieutenant Oliphant called in briefly. After he left, William pronounced, "Mistress Phemie, his father is a mere merchant. Such acquaintance must be coolly discouraged now."

Hoping to discourage him coolly, I asked, "Before or after they are wounded in our defence, sir? And my own father is a merchant also."

"You must learn to act as befits your future position."

He's abominable lofty, from his daddie's wealth & rank – & he'd never let me forget how gracious it was of him, to wed common wee me. I'd not wed him if all his teeth were diamonds.

Tho' Aunt still wants me to wed Alan, she's preening at gaining me a magnificent proposal. Wee Nellie disgraced us all by giggling (she knows my opinion of William) & Aunt whipped her for impertinence after he'd gone.

Thursday, 30th January

Cumberland has arrived in town. I saw him in a carriage, very tall & fat. He's staying in the Pretender's old rooms in Holyrood. He hasn't called in the Bailies yet, he must have heard how enthusiastic Edinbro was for the Prince.

Captain Mathieson called in with a note from Father – Mother's unwell & I've to go home. Aunt said, "We're sorry to lose ye, but of course ye must go as soon as ye can." Captain Mathieson says, wind permitting, he'll sail north again in 4 days, before Cumberland commandeers all ships to carry supplies for his army. Sailing again, dear Lord! But there's nothing else for it, if Mother needs me.

I'm sorry to go, but at least I'll no longer suffer William Needhold! He came to supper, very gracious, with a gift of a string of coral beads. When he heard I was going home, he announced he'd come after me as soon as he could (he means as soon as it's safe) to speak to Father. I repeated, it was my father's decision. And I'll make sure he refuses!

Sunday, 2nd February

Uncle says, "Stuarts never do the sensible thing!" For it seems the Prince is retreating north, even tho' he thinks he won the battle at Falkirk. Cumberland's left already, to join Hawley near Falkirk. Uncle says the armies will meet in the Highlands, maybe near Inverness. As well I'm going home – I know officers on both sides, & can help keep my family safe. I hope!

I've received parting gifts from many friends. To keep my mind off the ship's rolling, Lizzie offered me her latest copy of *The Female Spectator*. "You keep your journal. It'd be wasted on me," I told her. "I enjoy spectating, but people, not Natural Philosophy and Astronomy, & I'd never solve any of the puzzles!" Nellie gave me a charm of shells to keep off seasickness. I gave her William's lace trimming, & Ben 2 shillings.

Friday, 7th February

We were stopped twice by English warships to check we weren't carrying Jacobite goods, but Captain Mathieson had a permit from Cumberland to sail, & that got us by, no bother. I wasn't as sick as before – maybe Nellie's charm worked. But I do not like sailing.

The house is in a state! Mother's sick, & cold in damp, dirty sheets. The servants are near all fled & none to care for her & wee Willie except her maid, sour Tina. Her daft son Gibbie in the stable is useless and Father's man Calum is dour & unhelpful save at Father's orders. Half the household goods are stolen. Father's too busy with business to notice anything, fretting that the Jacobites are coming closer. I drove Calum out to fetch a physician, but none would come, with Father a Loyalist & the town so Jacobite! With Prince Charles's army approaching, his supporters grow more confident daily.

In the Warehouse Father's shelves are empty, & just old Davie McLean is left there. I told him to find us bacon, mutton, oatmeal & dried peas, & peat & wax to make candles, but Lord knows who will sell to him. Father scarce dare walk down the street for Jacobites muttering & throwing mud as he passes. Only the redcoats protect him & they're dodging stones themselves these days.

Monday, 10th February

The cough is settled in Mother's lungs, & Willie's coughing also. I'm painting their chests with tar oil to ease them. I went to Dr McIan myself, but he only waffled, "I'm too busy, make a horehound & ginger infusion, and keep your mother warm!" Our physician these 20 years, & still he refused to help! I had Gibbie break up old furniture for firewood.

Tuesday, 11th February

Maggie & Annie Main called, malicious as ever they were at school. To welcome me home they said but it was really to find out whether I was Loyalist or Jacobite. I smiled, "I know little of politics, tho' I enjoyed dancing with Prince Charles." That made them blink! "You danced with him? The Prince himself?" Maggie gasped. I tossed it off, casual: "Ach, aye! I was at 2 or 3 of his Assemblies. He's an excellent dancer, & most courteous." That should still their venomous tongues!

Wednesday, 12th February

Mother's cough is broken at last, thank the Lord. A cart of peat finally came so I can warm the house & stones for her bed. Willie's better too – the wee rogue was likely just copying her to get attention, & cuddle up in her bed for warmth!

Cumberland's marching north towards us up the east coast, destroying every house suspected of belonging to a Jacobite, furious at his Scotch regiments for not being harsh enough. Prince Charles's army's expected in town any day. Father says Lord Loudon, the King's General here, is as nervous as a cat in a flood, for Fort George isn't strong enough to hold against attack. I'm fair nervous, too – our house is just across the road below the fort walls! We can't leave, either. Mother's too ill to travel by road, & Captain Mathieson has sailed already – or we could have carried her south or up to Aunt Hannah in Tain. And who'd take in Father's family in this Jacobite town?

Saturday, 15th February

Father was out on business, Willie in bed thank the Lord, Calum out drinking. Just after sunset, Gibbie brought in a visitor. It was Alan, risking his life again, to see me.

My heart near stopped. We stood silent so long that Gibbie grew nervous. "Will I be throwing him out, mistress?" My lips smiled. "No," I whispered, "no." Then Tina stuck her head in, looked at us, gripped Gibbie's ear & dragged him out.

I don't remember much of that hour. Alan, sweet Alan. He said he loved me, but did I really want him to dishonour himself & not do his duty? I don't care what he does. The moment I saw him, I knew I loved him. He's my man, now & forever. I tried to say so & I was on his knee, kissing him, when Father walked in.

He didn't scold or look shocked – Tina must have told him Alan was there. He eyed us coldly, lifted his coat skirt at the fire to warm his bum, & considered us. "For your mother's sake – my wife's sister – I'll not have you arrested, Mr Lawcock." I clutched Alan's hand. Father took a pinch of snuff & sneezed like a cannon, as usual. "I take it you came to ask my permission to wed Phemie? The answer is no."

I'd expected it. "We'll wed without it, then!" Alan said, "We'd prefer your blessing, sir."

Father exploded again with snuff & contempt. "Would any responsible parent let his daughter of 15 marry a rebel, with nowhere to lay his head save his saddlebags?"

"I'd no' wed her till the fighting's over, sir," Alan

retorted. "But I'll no' have you nor any man say that I courted a lass underhand. I'm a riding officer, carrying orders for the Prince —"

"The Pretender!" Father snapped.

Alan hesitated a moment. "For Prince Charles, then, sir."

"For whomsoever! What will Lord Loudon do if he learns my daughter's consorting with rebels, eh? Do you want to get Phemie & her family hanged, eh? No, no. You'll leave my house this minute, & not return. And Phemie, I forbid you to see him again."

"Have I no mind of my own, sir?" I demanded.

He smirked. "Not in this house you haven't. 'Honour thy father & thy mother' the Good Book says. It's my right to have you hanged for blasphemy if you defy me!"

My jaw dropped; "You'd never!"

"Whether or not, lassie, I've given you the command. If you don't obey me, it's you must take the blame, not me!"

Alan left, as Father ordered, but to my astonishment, he was chuckling! "A right shrewd man, Duncan Grant, Phemie! If the Prince wins, your father will have his daughter wedding one of his officers, but if he loses, then ye'll be wedding the son of a wealthy

Loyalist lawyer. Advantage to your father either way! And in the meantime, while we're no' wed, him refusing his permission keeps him safe from Lord Loudon, & he knows I'll protect ye when our army arrives!" I hadn't realized.

We stood in the yard for another hour, & I never felt the cold.

When he kissed me & slipped away, I went in. Father was still by the fire, sipping mulled claret, a wee smirk on his lips. "Sly as 7 stoats you are, Father!" He glinted an eye at me. "Aye, aye, lass. And would ye have it any other way?"

O, Alan, sweet Alan!

Sunday, 16th February

What have I done? Oh, what have I done?

After kirk, Mother was asleep, I stitching by her bed, right above the parlour. Father came in with 2 redcoat officers & called me, but I was still angered with him & didn't answer. He must have thought I was out. They had discovered that Prince Charles had arrived at Moy Hall to stay with Colonel Anne Macintosh and were discussing a raid this very night on Moy Hall, to capture the Prince. I could hear every word thro' holes in the floorboards.

What should I do? If the Prince was to be captured, Alan's heart would be broken. Could I do that to him? But if Alan was to warn him, he'd escape. But then the fighting would continue, & men would get killed – maybe even Alan. What should I do? I'm loyal to the King, & to Alan, both. But Alan's here, & King George isn't.

Later, when Alan whistled for me in the yard, & took me in his arms, I told him. I couldn't betray his trust & love. He kissed me swiftly, & ran to warn Prince Charles.

I couldn't help it. Now I know why Alan follows Prince Charles. Love.

Lord forgive me, what have I done?

Monday, 17th February

Redcoats crept up on Moy House last night, but Colonel Anne's servants fired muskets & the Loyalists thought it was an army & fled, while Prince Charles escaped in his nightshirt. The whole county – the whole country! – is laughing at Lord Loudon. So would I be if it weren't so serious. Alan must have ridden like the wind with the warning. Father's furious, afraid. Loudon's retreating north, all his men & guns are rattling past as I write – just leaving a small garrison in Fort George.

I must hide this book well. If anyone sees it I'll be executed for treason – by either side!

Later

Father's gone. He came in in a hurry, ran up to the bedroom & slammed drawers about. I went in to stop him disturbing Mother, & found him & Calum packing saddlebags with spare clothes, & all our silver! He scarce glanced at me. "You'll be safe enough among the Jacks, with your lad, Phemie," he said. "But I'll not. Look after your mother!" He ran down to mount his pony that Gibbie had saddled ready. Willie ran out & Father just snatched the lad up before him & rode off – Willie laughing in astonishment, Calum trotting beside them, & my jaw fair tripping me. Sons are always more important than daughters! But I'm glad Willie's away out of it.

Father's a coward, but the Jacobites would likely hang him for supplying Lord Loudon's men, if he stayed. Stones are crashing on the shutters already. But I must stay, to care for Mother, right among the soldiers & all Father's enemies. Who's to care for me, save Alan? I'm scared. Pray the Lord preserve me, & all of us.

Tuesday, 18th February

The Jacobite army marched in, crowds of them, swarming thro' the town to wild cheering, all my friends out waving & shouting, just like Edinbro. I stayed in, kept the house closed up, praying no hothead would set fire to the thatched roof before Alan arrived. A crowd gathered outside, shouting & cursing & throwing stones. Mother was terrified. And me. Then a dozen clansmen trotted up & scattered them! The leader battered on our door. I opened it – Tina was too scared. He swaggered in – tartans flying, huge & fair-haired – grinning like a spinet, bowing like a lord & kissing my hand. Lachlan MacLean!

He was bursting with energy, his vigour near shaking the house, but he was gentle with Mother's frailty, which put him right in favour with me. He boomed softly, "Ye'll lodge me & some few of my lads here, Phemie?"

"We'll be happy to, Lachlan," I told him. "Aye, sir, we're grateful for your protection," Mother said, adding her welcome to mine. He winked, & kissed my hand again.

Mother's eyebrows rose in amusement. I had to stop her – & him! – getting the wrong idea. "I'll move in here with Mother, Lachlan. You & your men can sleep in the other rooms, & in the stable & lofts."

So now we have straw spread over all the floors for their beds, & wet plaids & feet stinking out the house, & how we're to feed them Lord knows. But at least we're safe from the mob – our former friends. But what will Alan say?

Later

Did I say safe? Lachlan told us, "You'll be clearing out of the house this minute, ladies, for we're attacking the fort!" I wrapped Mother in blankets & Gibbie carried her out to the kitchen behind the house, by the stables. The fort's 2 cannon are set to protect the main gate round the corner from us, & we're just too far for soldiers to throw torches on to our roof. The Highlanders are firing a wee cannon from the cliff above us, & muskets from our house windows, & redcoats on the fort wall are firing back, musket balls cracking & splatting on our stone walls! We should be safe enough here, but dear Lord, let it all be over soon!

Thursday, 20th February

The fight continued all day yesterday off & on. Mother's been surprising calm – past caring, she says – & she & Tina cooked broth for everyone. The Jacobite surgeons worked in the stable while men carried in wounded friends & their women nursed them – all jammed & jumbled in the bloody straw, amidst all the din of shots & shouting! I helped the surgeons – what else could I do? The men needed me. It wasn't like the wounded in Edinbro, with huge gashes and hands cut off by broadswords. The surgeons had to probe long pincers, deep, deep into wee holes to find & pull out musket balls. The men were incredible brave, not screaming or hardly, & then stumbling off on their wives' arms to their own camp, or even returning to the fight. One old man, shot in the belly, died in my arms. It's horrible to think back on. I was sick twice, with the stink & blood, but then too busy to think on it.

Fort George surrendered at noon. The redcoats are being marched out to the town jail. We can move back this afternoon, Lachlan says. What a mess we'll have to clear – but it can't be as bad as the stable, nothing could be.

Later

Dear Lord, I thought we were all dead. Fort George is blown up & the bang could have woken the dead. Stones came crashing in window holes & thro' thatch,

Mother was shocked rigid & big Gibbie screaming! Lachlan could have warned us!

Sunday, 23rd February

Prince Charles isn't well with measles or some say a pox, Lachlan tells us. His clansmen are right handy, though. They've cleared out the bloody straw from the stables, & mended the thatch & shutters. A rough job, with just strips of leather for hinges & oiled linen nailed up to keep out wind & rain, but it's better than gaping holes. They bring in a sack of oatmeal most days, & sheep, pigs & beef – stolen, aye, but we need the meat. Four wives cook for them all & Tina grumps at the strangers in her kitchen.

Alan arrived at last. He'd been sent with orders to Lord George's men who are heading for Fort William. He stopped on the doorsill, as Father had ordered, but Mother insisted she'd not keep her sister's son out. He's not best pleased to find Lachlan's staying here, tho' they're friends.

He whispered to me in private that he was too late with the warning at Moy. The redcoats were already near, & the Prince was leaving when Alan arrived. So I'm not a traitor! What a relief! He says Cumberland's bringing regiments home from the wars against the French in America. What's to become of us?

Wednesday, 26th February

Lachlan's away most of the time, raiding in the west, stealing cattle & burning Loyalists' houses. Thank the Lord for him & Alan, or it's we would have been burned out! Lord Loudon, & likely Father, have moved away north. Prince Charles's men are spread across the Highlands, & Alan's riding all over with orders. He calls in whenever he's passing. Or leaves a twig of whin on the dairy windowsill. "When whin's in bloom, kissing's in season" they say, & even this cold sleety spring there's always a wee blossom sitting brave in a sheltered corner. So I go out "visiting" & meet him down by the Ness Islands. He's that concerned for my reputation! Sweet lad!

Oh, I'm weary – with worry for Alan more than caring for Mother & running the house.

Sunday, 2nd March

Mother came to kirk at last. Everyone smiled at us. Lachlan & Alan's friendship outweighs Father's Loyalism. But it's hateful that the townsfolk turned against us so easily, & so violently.

Mistress Dunbar & 8 other Loyalist friends are sheltering in our attics – their homes have been looted & burned by Jacobites. It could have been us! Oddly, there's little trouble with the Highlanders' women in the stable. They seem to sympathize with us & are kinder than you'd expect. And the Loyalist refugees are too scared & subdued to want to fight. But what a tension in the house!

Monday, 10th March

The fighting seems to have stopped. Cumberland's still over in the east, in Aberdeen, with German & English soldiers as well as Scotch. Training them to stand against a Highland charge, Alan says. We're having parties every second day now, busy as Edinbro. I'm asked to sing the Jacobite songs I learned in Edinbro, & "God save the King"; the Jacobite soldiers laugh themselves silly.

A note from Father, slid under the door, says he's well. Willie's been left in Tain with Aunt Hannah, poor wee soul. Father complains that Loudon has 2,000 men, but keeps dodging the 600 Jacobites chasing him. Davie McLean found us window glass for the house somewhere, Lord bless him.

Sunday, 23rd March

Lachlan & a Jacobite force met & scattered Loudon's men 3 days back. I hope Father's still safe. Mackintosh of Moy is a prisoner. He's been given to his wife Colonel Anne to keep safe. She greeted him, "Your servant, Captain." He bowed & replied, "Your servant, Colonel!" Ridiculous!

Tuesday, 25th March

Prince Charles gave a ball last night, but not as fine as in Edinbro. He's recovered from his measles, but now many officers have it. He didn't know me, as Maggie took great delight in mentioning! It was irksome, but it's best if I've not been dancing with the Pretender Prince if – when! – Cumberland arrives with Hangman Hawley & his growing army. Lord George Murray is coming to rejoin Prince Charles here. Alan's pleased. He thinks little of the other officers, even when they're well!

Friday, 4th April

A French ship bringing gold has been driven ashore up north & Lachlan's gone off to rescue it, for the Prince has no money. He can't pay his men except in oatmeal, so they're turning to stealing. The Highlanders are so ragged they're stripping clothes off the prisoners in the jail.

Alan's limping badly. A musket ball pierced his calf 3 days back, but he says it's not serious.

❧

Sunday, 13th April

Alan's back from Elgin – very thin, weary & worn as a chewed mouse. I'm sore distressed for him, what with the bad leg. (I'm weary my own self – with strain & parties. Never thought I'd say that!) The Jacobites are falling back before Cumberland's advance, without fighting. "If the Prince had sent reinforcements, they could have hurt Cumberland badly at the river crossings!" Alan said, sighing in frustration. "There never was such an ill-considered, ill-organized escapade as this, Phemie, & so many killed for a vainglorious clown!" (Shocking, when the Prince was once Alan's shining hero!) "Geordie was right, he's a prancing peacock. Look at the officers he chooses – dreamers all, & sinful proud of their pedigrees, the touchy, cocky braggarts!" "Leave him," I urged, but he shook his head. "I can't. I wish I'd never joined the man! But I did, I swore to follow him. And the worth of a man's word depends on who gives it, no' who it's given to." A man's idea – but I suppose he's right.

His leg's swollen & looks gruesome. We've poulticed

& bandaged it, but it's no' healing right. He'll no' rest & let it mend. "There's many has far worse," he says. He finally told me how it happened. "Pure accident. Some clumsy gowk behind me dropped his cocked musket, and it went off. How could I tell anyone that? What would they say about the Highlanders?" "No worse than they say now," I told him!

Monday, 14th April

The war's back with us – so sudden it seems! Cumberland's in Nairn, only 15 miles away, with twice as many men as the Prince, they say, & the Firth's crowded with transport ships bringing him more soldiers & provisions. Prince Charles rode out before noon to face Cumberland, with flags flying & pipes playing. The town's seething with both fear & hope, & several folk who've been cold to us because of Father's Loyalism are sudden all smiles. Mother says, "Fair-weather friends, Phemie. Keep your distance."

There's no word of Geordie. I pray he & Alan don't meet, but his bitterness must have faded by now, surely?

Tuesday, 15th April

No news came all day – nothing. The waiting was terrible, till at sunset Alan limped in, grey & exhausted. Mother & I spread his coat on the hearth to dry & sat him down. He slumped in Father's chair before the fire with a bowl of broth, shivering & chittering. "Those Irish officers! They've convinced His Highness that the honourable way for princes to fight is face to face in full battle! He's picked a ground on Culloden Moor, which is flat & open, all wrong for Highlanders. We'll be cut to shreds by Cumberland's cannon & cavalry! And the half of it's bog, so we can't even charge! The Scotch officers begged him to retire into the hills where Highlanders fight best. Then he could have let our tired men go home to see to their farms, & gathered fresh men. But he'd no' listen! The harder Lord George urged withdrawing, the more stubborn the Prince grew! Then O'Sullivan sneered, "The Scots are good troops till it comes to a real fight!" After that what could we say?"

"No?" I suggested, but he said I didn't understand. True enough.

"We waited for Cumberland to bring out his men from Nairn. But he didn't, & I slipped into the town to find out why." (The fool, risking his life like that!) "It's his birthday, Phemie! Cumberland's! He's 25 the day, & he's given his army a day's rest, with extra ale & cheese & time to mend their equipment ready for battle the morn. And us out there, freezing & starving the lee-long day." He was near weeping.

"So the Prince invited himself & his cronies off to dinner at Kilravock Castle, & had a fine time, while the rest of us stood out in the sleet. And now he's gone daft, Phemie, for he's leading a night attack on the Loyalist camp at Nairn. With tired, hungry men, & in the pitch black – & no roads across the moor, Phemie, nor stars in this weather, nor guides! They'll lose their way for sure, & if they do find the camp they'll be too cold & starved & exhausted to attack. Ach, Phemie, it's madness! Lord George says it's a better chance than facing the redcoats on a level field the morn, but I think he's just putting a good face on it, too disgusted & wearied to argue longer! He sent me into town to find food. I've sent out 3 carts of meal, but whether they arrive… Ach, Phemie, I'm fair done! But I can't bide, I must get on." He rose to his feet, murmured, "Thank ye kindly, Mistress Grant!" swayed, & collapsed.

We stripped him, there before the fire. We had to cut off his breeches; the wound in his calf is evil, oozing stinking yellow pus. We pray it's not gangrene! The surgeons are all out with the army. I tried to remember what they'd done in the stable, but Mother put me aside. "Your hands are trembling, lassie, let me." She cut the swelling open with a kitchen knife & cleaned it, then stitched it like a stuffed joint, & put on an oatmeal poultice. Tina set hot stones in my bed & Gibbie carried him up. He's so deep, he never stirs when I change the poultice every hour.

Prince Charles will just have to fight his damned battle without him.

Wednesday, 16th April

Maggie called early on. "We're all going out to Culloden for a picnic to watch the battle, would you care to come?" You'd think it was a cock-fight. They'll regret it. Alan's still asleep.

121

Later, just after noon

We can hear cracks in the distance – cannons firing. Mother & I don't see how Prince Charles can win this battle. We're altering a coat & breeches of Father's to fit Alan, & smallclothes, to put in my box by my bed. I told Tina & Gibbie, "If any asks, you'll mind this lad's my cousin. He came here with me & was shot by a Jacobite by accident. He's been lying here sick ever since." Tina's drilling it into Gibbie – she knows how important it is. Our Jacobite friends won't tell, we hope. The local Loyalists have been away or keeping indoors. We pray they don't know of Alan – he's been around seldom & usually in the evenings, thanks to Father.

We've barred the shutters & doors. Lord protect us all.

About 2 hours later

Jacobite riders & men are fleeing past, screaming defeat & murder – the Prince has fled & the redcoats are coming. Alan's uniform is burned, the ashes thrown out & the buttons put down the well. Lord save us!

Evening

Everyone went out to cheer Cumberland's soldiers marching in with drums & flags, their uniforms red to the elbow & knee with blood. The church bells are ringing for them. As we returned, 4 Loyalist dragoons chased a Highlander down Castle Street & cut him down at our door, screaming. We had to step over him to get in. He's still lying there.

Alan's unconscious.

Thursday, 17th April

Alan's still asleep. Maggie's maid Ina crept in – brave to go about in town alone. Maggie's helpless with shock. The battle at Culloden was more hideous than she could imagine. She saw friends killed & a man & his young son both shot for nothing – just ploughing. Shots hit her carriage! Mistress Main has collapsed. Mother's gone out with Ina to help. They took Gibbie, which is better than no protection. She's not back yet – I pray she's safe.

Ina had more news. That daft night raid Alan talked of failed even to find Cumberland's camp. Many Highlanders just rolled in their plaids and fell asleep exhausted under the bushes, or went off seeking food. The Prince is fled, his army scattered. Only 50 redcoats were killed in the battle, but they say 5,000 Highlanders died. That *can't* be true – it's more than half the Jacobite army. Most of them must be fled. Lord George's regiment & some others managed to withdraw in fair order across the river and get away.

The streets are red with blood. The redcoats found the Loyalist prisoners half-naked & rat-eaten in jail & they're furious! Their sergeants are hunting among the Jacobite prisoners for deserters from the King's army, to hang them.

The Jacobite women have vanished from our stable.

Later

We're safe – I think. Redcoats came to our door, banging at it, & my heart near stopped. But their officer was Geordie! He's taller & seems older. A young man – even in 3 months – & no more a sulky laddie.

But was he still as bitter? Would he give Alan away?

"Phemie! Are ye well?" he said. "I've sought ye out special. We're patrolling, seeking fugitives from the battle. I wondered – I feared – he might be… With the Pretender being here—"

"We're all fine, Geordie!" I interrupted. "You're well yourself? There's none here that's a Jacobite. We had Highlanders staying here, but they're gone now, thieving rogues!" I hugged him, to grins from the men behind him. "Seek all over," I told him. "See for yourself, I insist!" Geordie nodded & waved his men to come in. "Just don't disturb Alan up above us." Geordie stiffened. I hurried on, before he could say anything. "Aye, your brother Alan, Geordie! You didn't know he was here? He escorted me when I came home." I stressed those words just a bit. "He was shot by a Jacobite – a ball in the leg. You've no' heard? We wrote Aunt Morag, but… It's bad, I fear me."

The sergeant sent men off to search the stables. I led him & Geordie up the stair. Mother was in my bedroom, stiff with fear. She scarce slackened as I introduced Geordie – she knew how he felt about Alan. She didn't trust her voice, just curtseyed to his bow & made herself smile. "Come in, then, but hush," I told them, for fear Alan would wake & say something

125

to betray himself. Geordie stood just inside the door, stiff & cold, glanced down at his brother, & then stared. "Alan?" he said. "That's never Alan. He's old, Phemie!"

"It's the pain," I said, & lifted back the blanket. "Mother, will you send Tina up with a new poultice & maybe find Geordie's men some ale? I think there's a drop left to us." She nodded, still wordless, & slipped away, while I unwrapped the bandages. "I'm feared of gangrene, Geordie. The wound's never healed, no' for all we can do, all this time. Look at it, you can see with that leg he couldn't have taken part in the battle. He's seen no fighting at all." The sergeant's face twisted in disgust at the stink. He was convinced. Geordie stood rigid, while my knees trembled.

Then Alan cried out in fever, "Damn the Prince! Bull-brained gowk! Curse him! Curse them all! Damn those Irish, & the Prince, & all of them!"

The sergeant laughed. "'E ain't no Jacobite, miss," he grinned. Geordie started, & huffed a breath, & nodded sharply. My knees near melted with relief as the sergeant stomped out.

Geordie watched in silence while I changed the poultice and bandaged Alan again. When I was done, he said, "He never fought against the King?"

"He's never lifted blade nor pulled trigger. He even missed Falkirk & he was shot by a Highlander, accidental. I swear it before the Lord, Geordie," I said. "He only stayed with the Prince out of duty. You heard what he said. He's fevered, so he couldn't have been lying. Look – I can prove it!" I showed him this journal, with Alan's words all written down. "I beg you, Geordie, don't betray him – & me!"

He studied it & nodded slowly, reluctantly almost. "Aye, right, then. It seems he's come to his senses." He sat down wearily by Alan's side. My hands were trembling as I hid the book again. "I suppose…" He grimaced. "It's no' easy, no' after thinking hard on him all this while… But there's those will mind on him joining the Pretender. They'll report him as a traitor. And after what happened to the men in Carlisle… We can't just leave it." He was thinking hard. "What ye'll do, Phemie, is this. Cumberland's issued a proclamation – all rebels must surrender their arms to the nearest magistrate or minister & submit to the King's mercy. Alan can't do it, so you'll do it for him. It's a risk, aye, but no one'll be hard on a bonny lass like yourself, I'm certain sure. Special when you can prove with that book that he's changed his mind a while back, & if he's never fought, & crippled & near dead. Ye'll swear to that, eh?" He glanced down. "I'd best come with ye to support ye & prove the family's loyal at the core... Aye, that's the best, that's what we'll do. We'll go to – who's the Provost here?"

"John Fraser, he's an old friend of Father's."

He looked down at Alan, bitter & yet resigned, Alan no' yet forgiven. Then he turned away briskly. "I must get on. I'll come by the morn, then, & we'll go together."

Thank the Lord!

Oh, is my hand no' sore with writing?!

Friday, 18th April

Provost Fraser's a feeble old soul, & worse in these dreadful times, but Bailie Hossack was with him, the last Provost, & he kept us right. He wrote down Alan's name & took his pistol & sabre. "Aye, well, lassie, there's a many villains about, far worse than romantic young fools like him. Bring him in when he's well, to swear loyalty to King George, & if he's no' wanted special for any misdeed ye'll likely hear no more of it. Eh, Provost?" Old Fraser nodded & smiled. I'm so relieved!

I hope I need never show this book again to anyone.

The jail's full, so they're putting prisoners into houses & cellars. About noon, 20 Jacobites were driven in to our stable with bayonets, their wounds not tended, their plaids stripped from them, & moaning unbearable for water. Mother told Gibbie to take them bread & water, but the guard stopped him. I went myself, but the guard knocked the bucket from my hand. "Only traitors helps traitors!" He spat at my feet, and would've done so in my face if he'd dared, but Geordie's protection covers me.

Later

Father's back. Willie's still with Aunt Hannah. It's sensible to keep him away from here, even Mother agrees tho' she misses the laddie. Father's full of vinegar against the Highlanders. When he heard about Alan, he stamped into my bedroom & hissed, "Jacks in my house? Are ye mad, the pair of ye? Get him out!"

Mother bristled, but it was me stood up to him. "He stays, Father," I declared, quite calm. (Proud of myself!) "He's honestly reported, as a former Jacobite who has repented his folly. He's in no danger, nor us for keeping him. And besides, I'm going to wed him."

He stared, dumbfounded, but I kept on. "See, Father, there's 3 things can happen. Either you use your influence to keep him safe, & when he's well I'll wed him, here, with your blessing. Or you ignore him, & when he's better I'll take him home, & I'll wed him in Edinbro without your blessing, & you'll never see me again, nor my children. Or you can use your influence to have him arrested, to prove your loyalty, & I'll go with him, with no wedding at all, to London or slavery or the gallows – wherever he goes. For he's my man & always will be. So, Father. Which will it be?"

He glared at me, & at Mother, & at Alan asleep & sick. "Or there's a fourth," he said. "He could die."

I gritted my teeth. "Aye, Father, he could die. That would save any further argument. But in the meantime, you decide whether you want me to be your loving, caring daughter, or whether you'd rather lose me for ever."

He stalked out unspeaking to inspect the Warehouse. Mother smiled, eyebrows up. "Aye, well! My wee lassie's become a woman, eh? Well done, my dear, just splendid!" We fell into each other's arms, weeping in relief & fear. I never thought I could talk to Father like that – I couldn't have done it last year! For my sweet Alan, though, I'd face the Devil himself!

I moved back into my wee room to a pallet beside my bed, away from Father. Alan's still fevered. When will he wake?

Saturday, 19th April

Cumberland held a victory parade in town, with Loyalist bands & cannon & soldiers. The Jacobite prisoners were there as well, driven out of their cells naked & wounded, & supporting each other as they staggered along. Disgusting. Cumberland, huge on an enormous horse, came last – glowering at us because we weren't throwing stones at the traitors. All my Jacobite friends were out cheering him. Scared not to.

Our stable's near as bloody & filthy as after the fight for the fort, with 3 of the prisoners now dead. I told Gibbie to take them on a wheelbarrow to the cemetery, but soldiers there turned him away, shouting, "Throw the dogs in the river!" Tina & I swept out the dirty straw, burned it & pulled clean down from the loft. We hid bandages, a bucket of water & a bag of oatmeal in a corner where the prisoners would find them.

We hear terrible stories about redcoats being sent to slaughter the wounded Jacobites on Culloden Moor & burning houses full of wounded men. Dreadful, if they're true. Cumberland claims Prince Charles gave the order to kill all redcoats. (I don't believe it, he was always gracious & generous.) So he & General Hawley are determined to kill all Jacobites.

The house is full. We have the prisoners & guards, & 4 of our Jacobite friends are begging shelter (after near spitting on us last month!). Even some of the Loyalist refugees are still here, since redcoats have taken over their houses.

Father's raging. The Warehouse has been looted by two armies & its shelves broken for firewood. He's ordered Davie McLean to have all in order for new stock within 2 days. Captain Mathieson must be due again & that cargo brought north with myself has been hidden somewhere – Father knows all the best places for that!

Sunday, 20th April

Last week, General Hawley had Bailie Hossack, the last Provost, & Provost Fraser kicked down the Courthouse stair for begging mercy for the wounded. Then Fraser was forced to muck out his own stable, poor old soul. The town's so full, prisoners are being stuffed into the holds of ships in the Firth. We have another 10 prisoners, brought to replace those who have died. At least we're let feed the men now – $\frac{1}{2}$ lb. dry meal daily, & Hawley says that's too much! Savage old man! His sergeants have found & hanged about 20 deserters.

Redcoat officers call on us to curse our prisoners as traitors. They jeer at their nakedness & how they have to use the fronts of their shirts to hold their oatmeal. When I went upstairs today after they'd left, Alan had wakened. He'd heard the swearing & threats of hanging & crawled terrified under the bed to hide! He's so weak & thin Mother & I could lift him back, but it was hard to persuade him to lie quiet & sleep again, for he scarce knew us. His fever's still high. He's often raving & even tries to rise & ride with orders. I get no sleep. The swelling is worse – Mother put a handful of maggots on the wound to eat away the dead flesh but they haven't worked.

To go on with life you have to grow a shell like a cockle to keep out what you can't bear, until you scarce notice it. Is that not the worst of all?

Monday, 21st April

Alan's very ill. Father ignores him totally, but at least hasn't had him arrested. Geordie's angered by Father's hostility. It makes him feel kindlier to Alan himself, in opposition.

The Warehouse is open again, tho' Father's the only merchant with much to sell. The Prince's Highlanders stole everything they could lift.

Lieutenant Oliphant from Edinbro called & says he's glad of friendly faces & a civilized cup of tea. He says many Highlanders gathered after the battle, but Prince Charles just sent them a message to save themselves & fled west! So they've all gone home. I pray that's the end of it. Of the fighting, anyway. Will it really ever end?

Tuesday, 22nd April

I fear Alan is dying.

Wednesday, 23rd April

Geordie brought in his regiment's surgeon – a hateful, rough man – half drunk & his coat all black with dry blood. He took one look at Alan's wound, called in 4 soldiers to gag & hold Alan, & took off his leg above the knee. I held Alan's hand as the man cut & sawed, very fast. Geordie says he's famous for it. It only took 2 minutes, Mother says, but it seemed ages, with Alan screaming & struggling, near crushing my hand till he fainted. Alan's leg thudded on the floor & the stink of blood was dreadful – far worse than anything in the stable, for it was that of my own love. I near collapsed, but I must be strong for Alan – he'll need me now. Oh Lord, what will he do? Even if he lives and he may not. The surgeon assured me, "He'll do fine!" but I can see he's doubtful. I'm praying for Alan every waking minute.

Sunday, 27th April

Alan's still alive, but barely. He scarce stirs when I change the bandages on his leg. I mean his stump – I must make myself accept it!

Two more dead bodies have been removed from our stable. I fear one was not quite dead yet. He squirmed as they heaved him on to the cart, I'll swear it! But when I protested the guard just laughed, "Save time later, miss!" he said. Horrible! And the beggars they hire to do the heaving are mostly starving Jacobites who have to earn their bread throwing their comrades into the river. We have 3 more Jacobites sheltering here from the redcoats.

There's typhus fever in town, brought by the ships from the Americas. Geordie told me dozens are ill, & some dead already. "It's kind you are to tell me. I'll be sure to worry about that as well, when I've leisure." He laughed & hugged me. "Never fear. Alan's tough, he must be. He falls with whatever's going around, but he always recovers." Please God it's true!

Captain Mathieson's away south again, carrying letters to Uncle & Aunt. I fear his ship is laden with goods the redcoats have stolen from local Jacobites. Father will be even more unpopular when our neighbours find out who's buying their goods, tho' who'll dare complain? He's fair bizzing about, shipping food down Loch Ness to the redcoat garrisons in Fort William & Fort Augustus, & buying the cattle & horses that they seize from Jacobites to drive south to sell in the big markets. Profiting from others' misfortune. I hate it.

Tuesday 29th April

Alan wakened & he knew me! He was still awake when Geordie called in & held his hand quietly for a while. Gladness shone from them both. Lord bless the surgeon & forgive my ill thoughts of him!

Geordie's going off west on patrol & says if anyone bothers us we're to go to Lieutenant Oliphant. The town's no' safe to walk in these days without an escort. Every second house is a tavern, & a wee girl was crippled last week by a horserace down the High Street.

There's 2 more prisoners lying dead in our stable. And we have 4 more Jacobites driven from their homes. We can scarce breathe in the kitchen. Tina's angered at the callousness of the redcoats & Gibbie's upset for the soldiers tease him. Mother's grim, not her normal lively self. It's a merry house this spring! I'm not that cheery myself, tho' I'm out often at parties. They're tiring, but better than sitting moping. I must go, for while the officers are friendly with me, Alan is safe. Some of them are incredible heartless, chortling about their men splashing Jacobite blood over each other at Culloden like children playing in a pool. The English ones loathe Scotland. "Damned eternal rain & fog, damned mountains ready to fall on your head, & damned rebels behind every damned rock! Can't relax, can't trust anyone!" they say. They should have stayed home, then.

Saturday, 3rd May

Cousin Alison came to the door today, half-naked & her bare feet cut & bleeding. We scarce knew her. She carried a babe in her arms & wee Anne & Frederick clung to her petticoat. Redcoats raided her house, smashed everything & found a broken old pistol in the back of a cupboard (maybe her husband's father's). They said it proved her man, Aeneas, was a rebel, tho' he's always been a good Loyalist. They'd no' listen, but just put him against a wall & shot him! They stripped & assaulted her, drove her & the children out & burned the house! She can scarce speak & just sits staring.

139

I pity the folk we've taken in. It's happened to them too, but you understand it deeper when it's your own family.

I asked Father to speak for Alison to Cumberland, for justice against her husband's murderers. He snorted. "Ye think I'm daft? Me, set myself against the master of Scotland? Such things happen in war. I'll see she gets a new house & gear."

"A new man too?" Mother said quietly.

Father just slammed out, & Mother sighed, trying to smile. "Your father's a hard man, Phemie," she said. "But he's doing his best for us."

"Best for his purse!" I said. She reared up like a startled cat. "Would you rather be poor, then? How would that help us? Or Alison? If we have wealth we can help our friends. If we haven't, we can't. And mind you this, my lass – nothing your father does is illegal. Sharp, aye. Harsh, aye. But within the law!" But does that make it right?

Today Alan sat up against pillows for half an hour. He's gaunt & pitiful weak, but Mother said, "It's your own doing, my lad! You would keep going, forcing yourself past your strength! But never fear. You'll be yourself in the end." If we can keep the typhus from him, that is.

Tuesday, 6th May

Half the redcoats camped down by the river are sick & so are the broken folk in the shacks all round them. They've come in from their ruined homes to beg from the soldiers. Shameful, but they're starving & their children are dying of cold & hunger, & now sickness. We have 16 refugees sheltering here now, & 4 are covered in red spots & burning with fever. It's definite typhus.

Alan has nightmares, crying out in fear over & over, poor lad.

Saturday, 10th May

Nine ill, 2 died. Alan has the typhus now & he's already frail. God help us all. Apart from the prisoners in the stable, there's 23 men, women & children crammed in our kitchen & attics now. Some are

Jacobites & some are Loyalists like Cousin Alison, driven from their homes & their sons, brothers, husbands & fathers shot for nothing, whether they're Jacobite or not. And Lachlan & the Jacobites were doing just the same to Mrs Dunbar & others, last month. Civil war, as Uncle Andrew says, is vile. I pray Geordie's not doing this.

Wednesday, 14th May

We struggle on from day to day, cooking, nursing the sick & carting corpses out to the big graves (20 or 30 bodies each) down by the river. Alan's very weak. Mother's a tower of strength, tho' ill so recent, & Alison also. They know medicines & charms, & keep the children busy. We've 26 refugees now – tho' 5 have died, & Alison's baby. She never mentioned it, just slipped out to the graves with it wrapped in an old petticoat, & back to work. Heart-breaking.

Father keeps clear. He's gathering silver as a fisherman catches herrings – & he stinks the same.

Tuesday, 20th May

Alan's spots are fading & his fever's down. He'll live, thank the Lord. None have died in 5 days, nor more fallen ill. Maybe the worst is past? I'm so tired.

Our refugees are all glad to be sheltered, but the women are snarling, "Traitor!" at each other & bickering constantly. And both resenting Father for doing well – & so Mother & me – & sniping that Alan's brother's a redcoat & so he's safe, when they've lost everything. Alan whispered, "I'm feared, Phemie! I hear them in the attic over my head, all day & night, cursing me, stamping & shifting to keep me awake." That finally snapped my temper! I reassured him it was a fever dream, then went down & blasted them all! "He's a good lad, & hurt, so from Christian charity you should wish him well. And I love him, & this is my house. You'll work together kindly, or every last one of you will go straight out that door & seek shelter where you may!" Mother frowned, but I snapped, "I meant it! And Father would support me, as he wants rid of them." So she scolded them as well. We can hope for peace now. Or at least civility.

Thursday, 22nd May

Captain Oliphant (he's been promoted) came to invite me out. Tho' I was weary beyond words, I agreed. Parties usually lift the spirits, but not this one. One Englishman said Cumberland recommends Jacobite clans should be trapped & shipped to the colonies as slaves, every last man, woman & child! A Glasgow man also told us that some Members of Parliament are fanatical, roaring that all Scotch seed corn should be destroyed, to starve us all to death & prevent another generation of traitors being reared here! Captain Oliphant said, "Aye, sir, & another fool says all Scotch women of child-bearing age should be killed. You'd think all Scots were Jacks!" "Ain't they, then?" the Englishman chuckled! After all we've been thro'! Another saw my face & laughed. "Never fear," he said, "we'd no' do that to a bonny lassie like yourself, Phemie!" "But if I wasn't bonny?" I said. They guffawed, but they would so. These callous louts are Geordie's friends? And Father's?

And I had to sing "God save the King" for them.

Friday, 23rd May

Alan's slowly improving. Poor lad, he's still easy alarmed & leaps awake at any sudden noise so that I must rise to comfort him. It's as well Father never thinks about the house. He's never asked whether Alan really needs nursing at night.

Cumberland marched off south today to Fort Augustus, leaving a garrison here, including Laurie Oliphant. To guard Inverness from a French landing to support another rising, I suppose. Our prisoners will be shipped south the morn, near 600 crammed in 7 small ships. Laurie says many will die & never stand trial. God preserve them. At least we can move the Jacobite refugees into the stable, leave the Loyalists in the attics, & get some peace at last.

Wednesday, 28th May

Captain Mathieson brought a letter from Uncle & Aunt, thanking us for caring for Alan & saying they're glad he's alive & Geordie's well. Edinbro ministers are all praising Cumberland's valour, thanking the Lord for his triumph over the barbarous Highlanders & the public blessings he & his family have conferred on mankind. Aye, maybe.

Father's home from Fort Augustus. He says Cumberland's determined to ensure Scotland never dares rise in rebellion again, & his men are eager to help him. The corpses of 9 Jacobite soldiers were found, stuffed down a well behind the barracks. The redcoats are in a killing mood, far worse than round here, even. They're not just English soldiers, neither. It seems more Scots fought against the Prince than for him, & they're taking this chance to carry on clan feuds.

Mother wants to bring Willie back but Father says he's safer where he is.

Thursday, 29th May

Gibbie carried Alan downstairs to sit in a chair in the sun for half an hour. I brought him out a cup of tea, & told him, "Gibbie's cutting you crutches & when your leg's firm healed he'll carve you a peg. I'll have you upstanding for our wedding!" He smiled a little, but then frowned. "It's no' possible, my dear. Thanks to your nursing & devotion, I'll live. But I'm no' a full man & I love ye too much to tie ye to a cripple, Phemie."

Just what I expected. I sniffed. "I never heard such blethers in my life. If you think for a single minute that you know better than I do what's best for me, you've another think coming, my lad! Even if you were right, which you're no', you can sacrifice yourself for your noble fancies if you feel obliged, but you'll no' sacrifice me!" He stared, dumbfounded. "I love you, too, Alan, just as you love me, & I'll no' have that despised! So that's it settled. We'll wed as soon as may be!"

"But I'm but half a man, Phemie—"

"So if we cut off the other leg you'll vanish? Away!

You're shorter in the one limb, but your brain's whole – or am I mistaken there? Which should I choose – life with nine-tenths of the man I love, or with none of him? You can study for a physician, & we'll do fine. Well, now you've got that gibber out the road – you have, have you no'?" He nodded, didn't dare not to! "Aye, we can get on, so. You've been out long enough. I'll call Gibbie." Then I whisked myself off before he could draw breath.

Give me up for my own good, would he? Gowk!

Friday, 6th June

Alan dressed for the first time. We had friends in for supper and when they left, I helped Alan to bed. We laughed & kissed as usual, & cuddled; & then... I've been dreaming about it for weeks. Oh my sweet, sweet Alan!

Sunday, 15th June

Last night, at first dark, Lachlan MacLean arrived, disguised in a decent poor farmer's grey breeks & plaid, come to see that I'm well! Mother says it's a great compliment, as it is, tho' he brings us into danger. I sneaked him upstairs to my room to talk privately. His arm was broken at Culloden, but he's hardy & it's mended well. He's still eager to fight! "We're never beaten so easily!" (Easily!) "We'll be setting the True King on his throne soon, never you fear! Most of the Prince's officers are safe – aye, Alan, Lord George is away! The Butcher—"

"Who?" Alan asked.

"Cumberland the Butcher! The name's well deserved, eh? Aye, the Butcher still fears us. He even offered Locheil a truce, & a pardon, if he'd stop fighting. What a damnable insult!"

"Cumberland offered to stop the fighting?" I gasped. "But Locheil refused? Why?"

Lachlan blinked. "Would you be having us make peace? You'd disgrace us!"

"My cousin Alison was assaulted by a dozen men, Lachlan, & her man murdered, & her baby dead, & her home destroyed – is that no' a disgrace?"

"It was the Butcher who did that, Phemie, not the Prince!"

"But he did it because you – Locheil – keep on fighting! If you'd stop, he'd stop! So you're causing it!"

Lachlan gave Alan that pitying look men share. "Ach, you cannot be expecting a woman to understand," he said & I near hit him. Oh Lord, are men all mad?

"Where's the Prince now, then?" Alan asked. "We heard he was off in the west," Lachlan chuckled. "Aye, it's among the Isles he is, waiting for a French ship to slip past the British Navy patrols." His face changed to grim. "The redcoat officers are seeking the Prince as if he'd murdered their mother, flogging & torturing to make the islanders betray him! But they keep their silence. True men even to death, Lord bless them."

"Are they all strong for the Prince in the west, then?" I asked.

"I fear not, Phemie. There's many are feared to take him in, & others tempted by the reward offered for him. £30,000! More than a man would see in 10 lifetimes – or in 100! But there's always some brave souls will risk their lives & homes to shelter him, & bring timely warning of danger."

Alan looked drawn. He still cares for the Prince despite all. "How is he in himself?"

"Gallant & debonair, they tell me. A true prince. He always rises to a challenge, the brave laddie."

"A sight too gallant for Scotland's good, I'm thinking!" I mumbled.

Not hearing me (maybe as well!) Lachlan chuckled. "It's not like a Prince he's living the now, tho'. He's eating plain oatmeal cakes, or trout grilled on an open fire, & sleeping in byres & caves. He moves on each day, fearing discovery or betrayal every minute. He's getting a taste for the whisky, for a dram's the remedy for morning stiffness! But the sooner he's away to France the better. I'm off there, too, to prepare for the next fight." He winked. "With grateful thanks to your father, Phemie, for a pass to travel, & a few shillings to earn on the way. These cattle he's bought from the redcoats, he's hired myself & some of my lads to drive them to Perth market."

Alan eyed him shrewdly. "Will they all reach there?"

Offended, Lachlan snorted, "Most certainly! A Highland gentleman's word is his bond!" Then he winked again. "But I'd not swear to it that a few beasts might not go missing from his other droves!" Serve Father right if they stole all his cows! "Well, I'd best go."

Rising, he kissed me (first time ever!) & chuckled at Alan's frown. "May the Lord bless you, Phemie, & Alan here, for I can see it's he has your heart, & there's little I could be offering you, with myself in exile." I checked no one was watching, & slipped him out.

When I returned, Alan was staring out my wee window. He turned, smiling at my worried face. "Never fear, love, I've no desire to follow the Prince again, no, nor help him, neither." He took my hand. "I've done my duty by him, & seen thro' his glamour. But I hope he escapes the hunters." He never mentioned that impertinent kiss! Sweet Alan!

He tires easy still, & fell asleep at once tonight, without even a cuddle. I've had time to write all this, for I can't sleep. What if the Prince does escape? Will he return, & the whole thing start over? Lord forbid!

꩜

Wednesday, 18th June

Alan hobbles about wonderful well on crutches, tho' he's still carried up & down stair. Gibbie's his slave, & runs for him far faster than for any of the rest of us! Alan jests, "It's my charming smile!" but I think he's right – it's charmed me, after all! I suspect Mother suspects us, but she says nothing. We shouldn't be doing anything – but we are betrothed, after all.

Sunday, 22nd June

Father's back again, from Fort Augustus. General Hawley wants to offer £5 for every rebel head delivered there, but Cumberland says no, it would waste public money. What a reason for refusing! They say the redcoats have earned £200,000 by selling stolen beasts. Prices are so low down south, Father has started renting farms to keep the cows for a year or so. It seems he don't care about the women & children from those farms dying on moors of hunger & cold, with every house for miles burned. Or about the crowds of starving, broken folk gathered round garrison camps licking up the blood & guts from cattle slaughtered to feed soldiers.

Two lads slipped in last night to find their parents, who are sheltering here. They've saved 3 cows & 8 sheep from their farm. This morn their father bought certificates from the courthouse to say they're loyal & to protect them from the soldiers. Then they left to try to rebuild their homes. I gave them axeheads & knives & needles from the Warehouse, to help them make new wooden foot-ploughs & tools, & re-thatch their walls with heather. I'll persuade Father to hire their fields to fatten beasts for him. If a few go missing, he can well afford it! Two families are gone to take ship for the Americas. I near wish I could do so.

Sunday, 29th June

Mother's scolding me for dreaming. I can't think straight. I'm carrying Alan's baby. It's only 3 weeks, but I know the signs. I'm a fool, I knew it would happen. Why did I risk it? What will Mother say? And Father? Half the lasses in the town are the same way, with the Jacobites & then the redcoats in town, & who can carp at them? Me – rich Miss Grant, Duncan Grant's lass that thinks she's so genteel since she went to Edinbro – I'm no different! All my "friends" will be eager to blame me & jeer at Father. The gossips would have me on the stool of repentance at kirk, while the minister preaches over me! Public disgrace – I'd rather die! What will Alan say? He'll stand by me, I know he will! I know he will.

Later

Alan's delighted! "My child! Ach, Phemie, there's nothing could cure me faster! Oh, but I love ye, my brave lass! And we'll no' go to London on our wedding tour. I'll take you to Italy, Milan, Florence —"

"No, you'll no'," I told him. "No' with this babe on the way. It'll have to wait a year or two!"

He insisted we tell Mother at once. "Ach, I thought so, you silly wee gowk!" she sniffed, shaking her head wryly. I should have known she'd know! "Aye, well. No need to tell your Father, he never notices women's matters," she said. "We'll get you wedded here as quick as may be, & then you'll go south, & who in either place will know whether the babe's a bit early?"

"Captain Mathieson's sailing the morn. With God's help we could get Aunt & Uncle here by my birthday, 16th July?" I suggested. "That gives us 3 weeks to get the banns read in kirk, announcing our wedding in proper form, so it won't look rushed."

"That'll be grand, Phemie!" Alan said, & kissed me.

At least I can wear my wee brooch openly at last!

When we told Father about the wedding, his jaw dropped. I laughed, that happy I could near fly. "We've been betrothed 6 months, after all! And we'll live with Alan's parents till his studying's done, & he can set up as a physician with a silver-headed cane!"

He finally snorted, "Aye, well, I've more sense than to try arguing with determined women! Sir Andrew's a substantial man, & well placed to set business my way. And the wedding will be popular here, & make my name better known." Trust him to find profit in it!

Monday, 30th June

Mother said, "Are you no' going to embroider your wedding linen, lassie?" I showed her 12 pillowcases, 10 towels & 8 sheets already worked with L's – for Lawcock – & she near split a seam laughing. "You did them in Edinbro? You've been that certain about Alan all along?" Near weeping with happiness, I just nodded.

I asked her if she loved Father when she wed him. She looked quizzical. "Love? Don't be daft. Regard, respect, liking, aye, but I was never a belle, nor he a ladies' gallant. But I was bonny enough, an' a good housewife. So I looked at the men around me, & chose the best bargain – a keen, steady, thriving trader. And he did the same. We've both got what we wanted. Your father has comfort & ease, & I have a fine house to order, silver to spend, & respect from every soul in the county. Maybe no' romantic, but it's practical – & on a freezing night, it's a feather mattress & a hot brick at your feet you want." She glanced sideways. "No' whin blossom!" There's no' much she misses! Better to have both, though.

Tuesday, 1st July

Sir William Needhold swaggered into kirk this afternoon! He'd sailed up & just arrived this morning. I near dropped when I saw him! He sat & smirked at me, till he heard our banns read. Then he turned white with fury! Everyone was staring in the kirkyard after the service, while he stormed at me in a strangled whisper. "I thought we had an understanding, mistress!" I had to stiffen my spine to answer him. "No, sir. I said no more than that you must ask my father." He went off in a raging sulk!

Alan wasn't there, tho' he's up & about quite steady on crutches. He's still easy startled. He'll get over it, but he's not fit for William yet a while. I wish we could just get married at once, but now the Minister's reading the banns, we must do things correctly or cause the disgrace we hope to avoid. Damn William Needhold!

Wednesday, 2nd July

William stopped me at market. "I spoke to your father, mistress, who declares that he would be most happy to see you as my wife!" Father sees the man's acres, no' his slobbery mouth! He's fled to Tain, keeping clear – but I'll sort him when he returns!

Officers came to supper, mourning my marriage, tho' they like Alan. "You prefer a Scot to fine upstanding men like us? Poor judgement, Phemie! Could do far better, a pretty girl like you!"

They tell me the Prince escaped from the redcoats in the Isles with help from Flora MacDonald, Lord Clanranald's daughter. She dressed him as a servant lass, carried him across to Skye in a tiny boat, thro' a storm & soldiers firing at them to a friend's house. When they found redcoat officers there, she held them talking while he was slipped away to a safe house.

She's been arrested, but the officers drank toasts to her health – she'll never be executed!

A lady of a good family guilty of helping the Prince is honoured whilst Cousin Alison's life is destroyed. Whatever happened to justice? Mistress MacDonald was brave, I must admit. I'd never have the courage to risk so much out of pure pity – & face such danger & keep my countenance. Last year I would have tried, maybe, for the excitement. But I've had enough to last me. A nice, peaceful marriage to Alan, & 6 bonny babies, that's what I want!

Friday, 4th July

Father brought Willie back from Tain at last. He's grown & glad to be home. (I don't blame the laddie!) Father's bought him a pony (stolen from some Jacobite farm, of course). Vile-tempered wee beast, it bit Gibbie's arm. But Willie loves it & named it Snipe. (Gibbie calls it Snap – first joke he's ever made! He's improving!)

160

I confronted Father about William Needhold. He tried to convince me I should wed him, "For ye'd be near the richest wife in Edinbro, & he's like to gain a seat in Parliament down in London!" I tore a right strip off him, till Alan crutched in & told me I should be more respectful to my father, which dumbfoundered me, & then tore an even wider strip himself!

"Sir, a father being aware that his daughter's devotion is wholly for a certain man, his natural fondness for her should persuade him to permit the marriage, unless the bridegroom were so lacking in worldly gear or of such disgraceful reputation as to be quite beneath contempt. Neither of which, I venture to assert, is true of myself. Besides which, it would be dishonourable to break your word, given already to her pledge made with me. And to force your daughter to wed a man she holds in abhorrence would earn the disgust & scorn of every man of sense & decency." Such fine language, I near burst with pride in him! Father was dumbfoundered too. I hope I don't have to tell him about the baby, as a final argument. It'd be better if he never learns.

Monday, 7th July

Our wedding was announced for the second time. Only once more! Sir William was at the kirk, sneering at the back. He came to the house after, but Mother said I had a headache & he didn't stay. Father keeps niggling about the financial benefits – next time he does it I'll blast his ears off!

All the women in the house are working in peace at last, stitching away at wedding finery. Mother has a tailor working in the parlour, making new suits for Father & Alan, & even Willie. Alan's suit is a fine dark grey broadcloth with deep silver braid on the cuffs & pockets, & square silver buttons. I'm changing the green ribbons on my fine Edinbro chintz dress for silver, to match him.

I hope Uncle Andrew & Aunt Morag arrive in time. Alan says, "It's in God's hands to send a good wind, Phemie. If we must, we'll wed without them. They'll bless us anyway." Sweet Alan! But I want them there! And William away! I'm daft as a wee bairn, thinking that if I wish it, it must happen!

Tuesday, 8th July

Today I told William, "Sir, even in Edinbro I'd no mind to wed you, but I didn't want to hurt your feelings. It seems you have little care for mine! You know fine well I'm betrothed to Master Lawcock & due to wed him in a week."

He leered. "I admire your lack of vanity, ambition & greed, Euphemia, in pretending to refuse the wealth & position I can offer you."

"There's no pretence about it, sir," I snapped, "I do refuse you! I'd no' wed you, no' if you had half of Scotland in your pocket! I'm firm determined to wed Mr Lawcock, sir!"

"But ladies are well known for changing their minds!" He bowed & left. Just as well – I near crowned him with a poker.

Friday, 11th July

The bully's calling in every day now, & if I deny him he stands outside glowering to make a scandal. The whole town's laughing at us! He's threatening me now; "Your father will command ye to obey him & wed me," he says, "& the Duke of Cumberland will insist on your submission to him, on the request of worthy gentlemen like your father & myself. Who'll disobey a Royal Duke?"

"I will! I'll never wed you, sir! D'ye think to make me love you this way? For if so, you've mistaken me quite!"

He just laughed & said it made the chase more interesting! Infuriating, that my opposition seems to make him keener.

Alan's a fine support. "My parents' word will be as strong as your father's in Cumberland's ear!" But I can't settle. Mother says it's just nerves, with the baby & all.

Some officers called in. They think it's a great jest, making bets on who'll have me! Laurie Oliphant saw me near tears, & soothed me by telling me they all like

Alan better. He's so kind! He promises all the officers will attend, & will allow no unruly interruption of the ceremony.

Saturday, 12th July

Father has returned to the attack, brandishing a gorgeous necklace of rubies from Sir William! I put the necklace back in its box (reluctantly!). "Pray you, sir, tell him I'm no' a heifer to be bought at market!" I said, & swept out. Man, did my fingers no' itch for that necklace, tho'?

Later

Aunt Morag's arrived. "Sir Andrew's laid up with cracked ribs," she told us. "The gowk fell on the stair last week – too much brandy!" But she brought messages of love and support from him & all my friends, & gifts too. Silver kid slippers & 4 silver plates! She agrees that William's a bully & Father didn't dare say a peep.

Aunt says Cumberland has recommended making Loyalist Glasgow Scotland's capital – not Edinbro that welcomed Prince Charles. All Uncle's friends are subscribing towards a vast silver dish to present to Cumberland. They're all desperate to show their loyalty to England's Hero, (the Martial Boy, as he's called) – specially those who most cheered the Prince! A new ballet about Culloden is wildly popular in London, with heaps of blood-stained Scots falling about the stage. Cumberland's income is doubled to £40,000 a year, in gratitude for saving Britain from the savages – that's us! And a new flower is named "Sweet William" after him – tho' we now call ragwort (that poisons cattle) "Stinking Billy"!

Sunday, 13th July

William Needhold yet again. I received him in the parlour, with Mother & Aunt & Alan to back me. He bowed. "Mistress, I'm come for the last time to ask ye to become my wife. Ye know well the advantages ye'd receive from this union with a reputable gentleman of rank & means, a constant supporter of the Government, & no' a traitor turncoat Jacobite." Alan stiffened, but sat still. "I give ye this final chance to accept my offer."

"And I give you my final refusal of it, sir."

"As ye will. I fear ye'll regret that decision, mistress." He bowed out fast, as Alan started to rise at the glowering threat. Ach, Hell mend the rancorous rogue, why should he harass me so? Are there no' other lasses who would be glad to wed his purse?

Monday, 14th July

Our banns were read for the last time in the kirk. Two days to go! William's left the town, thank the Lord. I pray he's away to Edinbro. But Geordie's back, & a Lieutenant now – promoted on the field! "I demanded leave, Phemie! Can't miss my brother's wedding!" He & Alan & Aunt fell into each other's arms, hugging & laughing & weeping with joy. It's grand to see them all easy together at last!

Tuesday, 15th July

We're all working like slaves to prepare the finest feast ever in Inverness! If I have strength to say, "I do!" the morn, I'll be lucky!

Wednesday, 16th July

I'm wed, I'm wed! I'm Mistress Alan Lawcock, & no sign of William, & all's well! Just 2 minutes to scratch down how happy I am. Sunshine, all our friends, & my dress fine, & Alan handsome & sure on his crutches, & Geordie as groom's-man, & all smiling. I'm that happy I could fly! The officers made an arch of swords for us as we left the kirk, & there was a vast crowd. The whole town was out to cheer us home. Just a glass of wine & time to scribble this, & now to feast & dance all night! Oh, am I no' happy?!

Later

We were dancing, with Geordie & I leading a Strathspey (the same as I danced with Prince Charles last year), when 2 men came in. William Needhold & a strange Army Major. They walked right through the hall & broke up the dance in confusion. "There he is," William said. Smiling.

"Alan Lawcock?" the Major asked. "Of the pretended Prince Charles's Life Guard? Ye're under arrest as a foul traitor."

I screamed that I'd reported him faithful, & Mother & Aunt & all the guests were shouting. "This is a wedding, can ye not see? Shameful. Damn your duty sir!" Alan was white in shock.

The Major yelled, "Are ye armed, sir?"

Alan wavered unsteady, reached into his pocket, & brought out my wee pistol that Uncle gave me to protect me. He must have found it in my box some day while he was so feared of attack & kept it. He held it out to the man. "Just this, sir. A wee pop-gun, just!" I never knew he had it.

Guards at the door had come in at the screaming. They saw the pistol in Alan's hand, & one raised his musket &

shot him. He died in my arms.

My Alan. Oh God. My sweet, sweet Alan.

22nd September, 1781

I came upon this journal while clearing out the attic. There being some space free at the end of the book, I shall finish my story.

William Needhold I never saw again, but I wed Laurie Oliphant that October. As Mother said, my child needed a father & it was the practical thing to do. He was a kind, good man, & I liked him, as Alan had done. We had 12 years in comfort & affection till he died, away in Jamaica – I shall never see his grave. He loved my son, Laurence Alan, as his own. We have 2 girls, Euphemia & Rebecca, both wed now.

Last year, Laurence married Isobel Milton. They went to tour Italy, & as company for Isobel for the 3 or 4 months, I went with them. I'd always thought to go with Alan.

In Florence, I saw Prince Charles again.

We went to the Opera House to hear "Don

Giovanni", a daft musical play. A while after it started, a drunk man, pasty & bloated in his pink satin clothes, started shouting from the Royal Box, & throwing bottles at the stage. The performers hadn't waited for him to arrive, nor stopped the play till he was seated.

This was Prince Charles. The Chevalier of Albany, they called him there. In September 1746 he escaped from Scotland on a wee French ship. He wandered around Europe for years, begging for money & men, & embarrassing everyone. They say he refused the crown of America as it was businessmen who offered it, not nobles. He married a young Austrian Princess, Louise of Stolberg, but she said he was constant drunken. He bullied & beat her, & last year she ran away with a poet. Small blame to her.

He never wrote to thank Mistress MacDonald nor none of the others who helped him & suffered for him. He never paid Lochiel's expenses, as he'd promised, nor anyone else's. He refused to meet Lord George ever again, tho' my lord was exiled for life for him. He never again saw his father in Italy, nor even sent a letter, before the poor old man died. His brother & the Pope pay him a pension, & Jacobite clansmen still gather pennies for him after paying their taxes, tho' it means suffering hunger & cold & hardship. He spends the money on fine clothes, women, gambling & drink.

Cumberland died in 1765, too fat to ride & still known as the Butcher.

Prince William, Duke of Cumberland. Prince Charles Stuart, Chevalier of Albany.

Aye, it was the Duke's soldiers, Scotch & English, who wrecked Scotland & shot my Alan, trying to keep the crown safe for his family. But if Prince Charles had never been ambitious for the crown himself, there would have been no reason for all the destruction & misery. May God curse both the two of them!

Alan, my sweet Alan.

Historical Note

In 1685, King James VII of Scotland and II of England was crowned. He was a Catholic, and there was a certain amount of opposition to his rule because both countries were mostly Protestant. However, those who feared another Catholic monarch after James could take comfort in the fact that his Protestant daughter Mary, married to William of Orange and living in Holland, was the next in line to the throne.

Then James VII and II remarried and in June 1688 his son, James, was born. This meant that James would become the English and Scottish monarch after his father's death, instead of his half-sister Mary. The prospect of another Catholic king worried enough people in high places to prompt the "Glorious Revolution" – William of Orange arrived in England in November 1688 and announced that he and Mary were now King and Queen instead of James VII and II or his son.

King James fled to France, where he did have some supporters – France was a Catholic country with a history of war with England. James hoped that they would help win him back the monarchy of England and Scotland. These French supporters called themselves "Jacobites" after the Latin for James, *Jacobus*. When the old King James died in 1701, the Jacobites continued to support his son, calling him King James VIII and III. To supporters of the new monarchy of William and Mary in England, James was known as "The Pretender".

The French Jacobites hoped that the Highland chiefs of Scotland would help them fight to put James on the throne in place of William and Mary. Unlike the people who lived in the Scottish Lowlands, the Highlanders were made up of separate clans ruled by chiefs, spoke mainly Gaelic, and dressed in tartan blankets known as "plaids". They were fiercely proud of their military traditions and history. In fact, most of the Highland clans either remained neutral or supported William and Mary, but some did agree to fight for the Jacobite cause.

The Scottish Jacobites' first uprising was led by John Graham of Claverhouse in 1689 against King William's army in a battle at the Pass of Killiecrankie. The Highlanders won the battle, but many of their men were killed, including Claverhouse. The Jacobites were defeated in 1690 at Cromdale.

King William wanted to make sure he would have no more trouble from the Jacobite Highlanders. His most brutal act of vengeance was the massacre of 38 men, women and children of the MacDonald clan at Glencoe. This added more support to the Jacobites' cause.

Anne became Queen of England and Scotland in 1702. The English and Scottish Parliaments created a joint parliament for both countries and a new country called Great Britain. Despite the huge unpopularity of this measure in Scotland, the English Parliament made sure the vote for the Union was passed via a combination of threats and bribery. Riots broke out in Scotland when the Act of Union became law in 1707.

The French King, Louis XIV, saw the Scottish people's dissatisfaction with the new Parliament as a chance to cause unrest, which would be useful to him in the war that was going on between Britain and France at the time. James ("The Pretender") was still living in France, and in 1708, a year after the Act of Union was passed, Louis XIV gave him ships and soldiers to help win back the kingdom he'd left in 1688. The attempt failed miserably: James was ill and the French fleet turned back when they were attacked by the British Navy. James didn't even manage to set foot in Scotland.

In 1714 Queen Anne died. Since Anne had no surviving children, her heir was a distant relative, George, Elector of Hanover. Many people in Scotland didn't support the new monarch, who had lived all his life in Germany and couldn't speak English. Support for the Jacobites was now greater than ever, and another uprising was planned.

"The '15" uprising was led by John, Earl of Mar, whose army of between 12,000 and 20,000 Jacobites fought King George's troops at Sheriffmuir. The results of the battle were inconclusive, but the news that another Jacobite army had been defeated in England (there were two Jacobite uprisings in England at the time), added to the shortage of food and money, meant that the Jacobites at Sheriffmuir simply gave up. Shortly afterwards, James arrived in Scotland, where a coronation was planned. But by this time, the Jacobite army had all but dissolved. James went back to France, leaving Scotland for the last time in February 1716. A further Jacobite uprising in 1719, this time with help from the Spanish, was quickly crushed. But despite a history of defeats and disappointments, support for the Jacobites remained.

In 1744, when George II was king, Britain and France went to war again. By this time, James had two sons, the eldest of whom was Prince Charles Edward Stuart, known as "The Young Pretender" and better known today as "Bonnie Prince Charlie". Charles travelled to Paris and persuaded the French King Louis XV to help him in a new Jacobite rebellion. Charles was given a fleet of ships, which were wrecked in a storm before they could set sail for Scotland in yet another Jacobite disaster. Undaunted, Charles sailed to Scotland with just two ships (one of which, carrying all Charles's weaponry, was damaged and had to return to France). He arrived in the islands of the Outer Hebrides with just seven supporters, no army or weapons, and very little money. Charles managed to persuade some of the Highland clans to support him (although many did not, and there were divisions of loyalty even within families), promising French help later, and gathered the Scottish Jacobite clans together.

The Jacobite army succeeded in capturing the capital city of Edinburgh, where Charles's father was proclaimed King James VIII and III to cheering crowds. King George's army of redcoats, led by General Cope, marched to meet the Jacobites. Just outside Edinburgh, the Battle of Prestonpans was fought and very swiftly won by Charles's army. Now

Charles controlled Scotland, even though many Scots, particularly the Lowlanders, did not support him. Charles's army marched south into England, so that he could finally put his father on the throne of both countries.

The Jacobite army captured the English town of Carlisle and got as far south as Derby. Despite being promised English support, only 250 Englishmen had joined them, so the army was still quite small. Since it seemed certain that large numbers of King George's soldiers were preparing to attack, the Jacobites returned to Scotland.

As the Jacobites retreated northwards, the Duke of Cumberland (George II's son) followed with his army and recaptured Carlisle. Meanwhile, Charles's Jacobite army, led by Lord George Murray, was forced into a battle with Loyalist troops led by General Hawley near Falkirk. Here the Jacobites managed another victory, although they failed to capture the city of Stirling. Charles and the Jacobites retreated to the Highlands, still pursued by the Duke of Cumberland.

The two armies met at the Battle of Culloden, the last battle to be fought on British soil. Cumberland's army consisted of seasoned English war veterans and a large contingent of Scottish men, all of whom were well fed and fairly well rested. Charles had run out of money and the French help he had promised showed no sign of arriving. His army, consisting mostly of Highlanders, was tired, cold and hungry, and outnumbered by at least two to one. The Jacobites were soundly and quickly beaten. The men in the victorious army were under Cumberland's orders to kill all the captured and wounded soldiers. They succeeded in killing many civilians as well. Cumberland earned himself the name "Butcher Cumberland".

After his terrible defeat Charles decided to give up. Butcher Cumberland's army marched through the countryside looking for Jacobite sympathisers and brutally killing them, burning their houses and crops. Some people who were in fact loyal to King George lost their homes and livelihoods at the hands of Cumberland's men.

Prince Charles fled, seeking shelter all over the Highlands. He famously evaded capture by disguising himself as the maid of a Highland lady, Flora MacDonald, who sailed with him to the island of Skye. Having been on the run for five months, Charles finally sailed away from Scotland forever in September 1746.

King George's Government passed laws against all Highlanders (even though only some of them had fought for the Jacobite cause), banning their Gaelic language, the wearing of tartan and the traditional Highland plaids, punishing any Highlander caught with a weapon, removing power from the clan chiefs and even banning bagpipes (which were seen as "weapons of war").

Even though Prince Charles's '45 uprising had left many people dead and led to the persecution of the Highlanders, some Jacobites remained loyal to the cause and Jacobite spies were active throughout the Highlands.

James, the Old Pretender, died in 1766, and Charles began calling himself King Charles III. He did not find many supporters during the last chapter of his life, however, and was well known for drinking too much. Prince Charles died in Rome in 1788. He left no children to carry on his claim to the throne of Great Britain. The Jacobite risings were finally over…

Time line

1603 Elizabeth I dies with no heir, and James VI of Scotland also becomes James I of England. It's the first time a monarch has ruled over both countries, although Scotland and England still have separate parliaments.

1625 Charles I becomes King.

1649 King Charles I is executed and Oliver Cromwell runs the country until 1660.

1660 Charles II comes to the throne.

1685 James VII of Scotland and II of England is crowned.

1688 William and Mary take the throne, and James flees to France.

1689 The first Jacobite uprising takes place: the Battle of Killiecrankie.

1701 James VII and II dies, leaving his claim to the throne to his son James.

1702 Anne, the last of the Stuarts, is crowned Queen of England and Scotland.

1707 The Act of Union is passed, which states "That the Two Kingdoms of England and Scotland shall ...

forever after be United into One Kingdom by the name of Great Britain." The Union is particularly unpopular in Scotland.

1708 James, "The Pretender", attempts to reach Scotland with a French fleet but is driven back.

1714 Queen Anne dies and her German second cousin's son, George, becomes King.

1715 A Jacobite uprising is led by the Earl of Mar. Despite an inconclusive result at the Battle of Sheriffmuir, the Jacobite army gives up. James does reach Scotland, but returns to France after only a few weeks.

1719 Another Jacobite uprising, with Spanish support, culminates in the Battle of Glenshiel, won by the Government army.

1720 Prince Charles Edward Stuart is born on 31 December in Rome.

1727 George II comes to the throne.

1745 Prince Charles lands on the island of Eriskay in the Outer Hebrides on 23 July. He captures Edinburgh and the Battle of Prestonpans is fought and won by the Jacobite army on 21 September.

1746 The Battle of Culloden takes place on 16 April. Charles's Jacobite army is defeated, and Charles finally leaves Scotland in September.

1766 James Francis Edward Stuart, "The Old Pretender", dies.
1788 Charles Edward Stuart, "Bonnie Prince Charlie", dies in Rome.

Few know my Face, tho' all Men do my Fame:
Look strictly, & you'll quickly guess my Name:
Through Deserts, Snows & Rain I made my Way,
My Life was daily risqu'd to gain the Day!

Evil be to them that evil think.

Charles Edward Stuart. To the Loyalists he was the Young Pretender, to his Jacobite followers he was known as Bonnie Prince Charlie.

J. M. Ardell Delinet Fecit

His Royal Highness

WILLIAM Duke of CUMBERLAND.

London Printed for John Ryall at Hogarths Head in Fleet Street.

William, Duke of Cumberland, was George II's son and a general of his army. He was nicknamed "the Butcher" because of his brutal treatment of the defeated Jacobite army.

The Prince and his Highlanders entering Edinburgh after the battle of Prestonpans.

A map of Scotland showing many of the places mentioned in this book.

*Flora MacDonald helped the Prince escape to the Isle of Skye in June 1746.
She was arrested but was released without trial a year later.*

Inverness during the eighteenth century.

The High Street, Edinburgh, from the Lawnmarket.

Edinburgh Castle and the Nor' Loch in the Eighteenth Century. The Loch was drained shortly after the Rising and parts of Edinburgh's New Town were built on the site.

SECOND DRAGOON GUARDS.
1780.

A Soldier in the Second Dragoon Guards.

UNIFORMS OF THE BRITISH ARMY, 1742.

Two British infantrymen.

Picture acknowledgments

P 184   Charles Stuart The Young Pretender, Unattributed Engraving, Mary Evans Picture Library

P 185   William Augustus, Duke of Cumberland, J Mc Ardell, Mary Evans Picture Library

P 186   Charles Edward Stuart and his Highland army enter Edinburgh in triumph after the battle of Prestonpans, after T. Duncan, Mary Evans Picture Library

P 187   Map of Scotland, András Bereznay

P 188   Flora MacDonald, after a painting by A Ramsay, Mary Evans Picture Library

P 189   Inverness from the west, Mary Evans Picture Library

P 190   High Street from Head of West Bow, Lawnmarket, WL Leitch, Mary Evans Picture Library

P 191   Edinburgh Castle and the Nor' Loch, Alexander Nasmyth, The National Gallery of Scotland

P 192   Member of the Second Dragoon Guards, Illustration in J Playford's Regimental History, Mary Evans Picture Library

P 193   Two British infantrymen, Mary Evans Picture Library

My Story.

the hunger

The Diary of
Phyllis McCormack, Ireland 1845-1847

10th November, 1845

Horrible! Horrible! The rot has destroyed most of the potatoes which were wholesome and sound when we dug them out of the ground. Da opened up the pit this morning and found it filled with nothing but diseased mush. All we have left to eat are those that hadn't yet gone underground.

"Six months provisions are a mass of stinking rottenness. Where has it come from?" Da kept repeating all morning. "Disease will take us all," he drawled.

⌇⌇⌇

My Story.

VOYAGE ON THE GREAT TITANIC

The Diary of
Margaret Anne Brady, 1912

Monday 15th April, 1912

It was after midnight, and I could still hear people
moving about in the passageway. Before I had time to go
out and join them, there was a sharp knock on my door.

I opened it to see Robert. His eyes looked urgent.

"Good evening, Miss Brady," he said. "You need to put
on something warm, and report to the Boat Deck
with your life belt."

Miss Brady? When I heard that, I felt alarmed for the
first time. "A routine drill," he said. "No need to fret."

I knew he needed to get on with his duties,
so I found a smile for him and nodded...

"You'll not want to take your time, Margaret,"
he said in a very quiet voice.

It did not seem possible, but maybe this was not a drill.

My Story.

BLITZ

The Diary of
Edie Benson, London 1940-1941

Friday 30th August, 1940

Last night was very still and clear. As Dad went
out for the evening shift, he looked up and said grimly,
"If they're ever going to come, it'll be on a night like this."
And sure enough, the first air-raid warning came at a
few minutes past nine. Mum was out at the ARP post,
and Shirl, Tom and I were huddled together in the
shelter with Chamberlain.

Shirl's teeth were chattering already. "Cor blimey!"
she said. "What's it going to be like in the middle
of winter? I've got no feeling in my toes at all."

I could see Tom was about to open his mouth and say
something clever when we heard the first explosion,
and then two more following close on the first one...

〜〰〜

My Story.

The Crystal Palace

The Diary of
Lily Hicks, London 1850-1851

17th April, 1850

The Crystal Palace is more wonderful every time we go, with coloured light everywhere, so airy and delicate, but strong. Not like a house, solid and heavy and shadowy, solid to the ground. Like being inside a diamond it is, or a fairy palace. Master has made a miracle, everybody says so. And as for the exhibits inside, there are more and more every day, 10,000 they say. We saw French and Belgian lace and English embroidery today, so fine the Queen can't have better – shawls and baby gowns and waistcoats, and Irish double damask tablecloths with shimmering ferns and flowers woven in. I was near crying with pure delight it was all so lovely.

My Story.

TWENTIETH~CENTURY GIRL

The Diary of

Flora Bonnington, London 1899-1900

22nd December, 1899

Time is marching forward, carrying us over the
threshold and pitching us, willy nilly, into a new
century. The prospect of growing up in that unexplored
territory is so thrilling that I fancy, if I close my
eyes tight, I can almost see the process taking place!
A day slips away like sand in a sand glass and then
another day dawns and so we are caught up in this
inevitable passage towards 1900. I bought a journal
and have begun to transfer all my scribblings of the last
few days into it. It will record my journey into the new
century. I shall call it "Twentieth-Century Girl",
for that is what I intend to be!

My Story.

My
Tudor Queen

The Diary of

Eva De Puebla, London 1501-1513

4th November, 1501

I hardly like to make a mark on the beautiful,
blank pages of this book, but I must. Mama gave it
to me as a parting present so that I could write about
this journey from Spain to England. "Don't waste it,"
she said. "Just write the important things." I'm sure
Mama would be impressed by the great procession in
which we have slowly made our way from the West
Country to London. Horses and carriages, litters and
baggage-waggons and attendants, soldiers, courtiers,
ladies, pages, jesters – and Catherine herself,
Catherine of Aragon on her way to wed Prince Arthur,
eldest son of the king of England.

꧁꧂

My Story.

The Great Plague

The Diary of
Alice Paynton, London 1665-1666

July 3rd 1665

Aunt Nell came home from the market looking very pale. She overheard two men discussing the Weekly Bills of Mortality. It seems that in the past week 700 people have died from the plague. So the plague is well and truly come to London after all. After much discussion I am to be sent to Woolwich with Aunt Nell. I refused to go without Poppet and Papa has relented. I was sent to enquire of a carrier but was soon stopped in my tracks. One of the houses in the next street had a red cross painted on the door. Above the cross someone had chalked "Lord Have Mercy Upon Us".